THEY WERE TRAPPED IN A WEB OF PASSION AND POWER, FIGHTING FOR THEIR LIVES!

Vicki Giotti: She hated her policeman father, yet vowed to avenge his murder, driven by a compulsion as dark as the day her mother disappeared. Now a second generation would play out a vendetta they barely understood—in the name of the law . . .

Arianna Tucci: The Don's darling daughter, she dared to rebel, to succeed in a career of her own. But danger would shadow her every move, from the white heat of desire to the black pit of revelation, as she reached out for love with no holds barred . . .

Francesca Cella: She left her daughters in the name of love. And in the name of love she returned to bring her daughters together and tell them the unspeakable truth. One woman, betrayed by two men, risking her life for the daughters she barely knew . . .

BLOOD SISTERS

BLOOD SISTERS

ROSEMARIE SANTINI

POCKET BOOKS

New York   London   Toronto   Sydney   Tokyo   Singapore

An *Original* Publication of POCKET BOOKS

POCKET BOOKS, a division of Simon & Schuster Inc.
1230 Avenue of the Americas, New York, NY 10020

ISBN: 0-671-67399-8

First Pocket Books printing March 1990

10 9 8 7 6 5 4 3 2 1

POCKET and colophon are registered trademarks of
Simon & Schuster Inc.

Printed in the U.S.A.

for my sister,
KATHLEEN

Special thanks to Cynthia Frazier

PART I

NEW YORK CITY

Late Summer
1988

✤ Chapter 1 ✤

Defendant sentenced to five to fifteen, years.'' Judge Rafferty said. As his voice droned on the courtroom became restless. Finally his gavel announced that the case was over.

It had been a sensational trial. The media had a field day as their cameras recorded John Hammer's baby-blue eyes protesting his innocence.

Sitting at the prosecution table, Vicki Giotti thought of the childhood song. What are boys made of? Frogs and snails and puppy-dog tails. In the eighties, she could add psychopathic behavior. What are girls made of? Sugar and spice and all things nice. In the eighties, in both the Chambers and Porto defense strategies, women were again being blamed when men killed them.

''Well, partner, we did it.'' Vicki's associate, Vito Marchese, shook her hand. ''We got the bastard.''

3

Vicki smiled. They had worked day and night on this case, and it felt good to be victorious.

"Now for Tough Tony Tucci," Vito whispered.

Her pained expression conveyed how deeply his reference to her father's murder affected her. Then a forced smile appeared on her face as she picked up the files and stashed them in her attaché case.

"Want to have dinner to celebrate?" Vito asked.

"Typical Italian," she laughed at him. "Eating to celebrate. No, thanks. I'm for a warm bath tonight."

"With a date, I hope," Vito flirted.

His eyes were warm and soft brown and reminded Vicki of a puppy dog.

"Maybe," she teased.

She tugged at her skirt. She liked short skirts because they bared her shapely legs. Above the skirt Vicki wore a collarless plaid jacket. Underneath the jacket, matching the gray skirt, was a pleated blouse. Her shoes were daring for the courtroom. Generally, she wore simple, low-heeled shoes in sturdy colors. Today they were gray polka dot and brought a smile to Vicki's face because they were cheerful.

She'd always loved shoes, even as a little girl, when she wore her pretty Mary Janes to bed. Her shoe collection was her secret vice. She had more than three dozen pair crowding her wall-to-wall closet. Having many pairs seemed safe; it meant she could escape anytime.

"Are you asleep?" her father called from the bedroom door.

Vicki hid her face under the blanket. It was cold in the small narrow room that overlooked Hudson Street.

On the walls were drawings from her art class. Her teacher, Sister Maryanne, said that Vicki had talent.

"Vicki?"

Her father's voice was coarse, the way it was when he drank too much whiskey.

She hugged herself, trying to stop the trembling. Her flannel nightgown usually felt cuddly, except on the nights when her father called out to her. Her Mary Jane shoes felt tight. When she rubbed the shoes together the hardened surface reassured her.

If he came too close, she could jump out of bed. If she managed to push past him, she could run to her Aunt Tillie's apartment next door.

Her father staggered into the small room.

"Hey, did you hear me call you?" he screamed.

He looked at her, his bloodshot eyes mean and dispirited. She peeked at him from under the blanket, trying to figure out whether this was a bad time.

It looked bad.

"Did you hear me?" he screamed again.

He stared at the wall drawings, then ripped one into shreds.

She trembled.

Looking around the bedroom, he spotted her favorite doll.

Not Cindy, she prayed.

He picked up the doll and yanked its artificial hair from the skull. The doll looked terrified without the lovely red curls.

Repeatedly he smashed the doll against the wall until the floor was covered with its shreds.

He moved to the bed.

Like a panther, she jumped past him. Her surprise

move unbalanced him, and he fell against the bed-post.

She ran to the door. In his drunken stupor he'd left it open. Her Mary Jane heels clicked as she ran to Aunt Tillie's.

"Aunt Tillie, please let me in!"

She prayed her father would stay on the bedroom floor. Sometimes that happened. On the lucky nights.

"Who is it?" She heard Uncle Larry's voice. Aunt Tillie's husband was a light sleeper.

"Let me in."

The door opened, and she ran inside.

"Shut the door. Quick."

"Vicki, calm down," Aunt Tillie said from the bedroom doorway.

She was a slim woman, gaunt though she was barely thirty. Like her brother, George, Tillie had slumped shoulders.

Vicki ran into her aunt's arms.

"There, there."

"He's going to hurt me! Please let me stay here. Let me live with you. I'll be good, I'll do the dishes, I'll sweep the floor, I'll make the beds, I'll . . ."

Uncle Larry looked at Vicki with dismay.

"You know that's impossible," he said coolly.

"Pretend I'm your daughter. You don't have any children. Please?"

"Vicki, you're almost six. You're going to school. You're grown up. You can't make up fairy tales," Aunt Tillie warned.

"Let me stay here for tonight," Vicki pleaded.

"You know your father. He'll take it out on us. Come on, I'll take you back."

"No!" Vicki shrieked. "I won't go back. He'll hurt me. Please!"

"Don't be silly," Aunt Tillie said impatiently. "Your father loves you."

"What about this?" Vicki pointed to a bruise on her left cheek.

"That was an accident. Your father had too much to drink. Come on now." Aunt Tillie pushed Vicki toward the door.

Vicki hugged her aunt, trembling.

"Please don't make me! Let me stay, please!"

Whenever Vicki worked on cases like Hammer's, in which a man victimized a woman, she felt deep sympathy for the victims. Like them, Vicki felt a powerful connection to the man who abused her. There was always love before the abuse began, which confused the victims. With children it was even more difficult to distinguish, for they did not understand that they could fight back.

When she was sixteen Vicki fought back. She celebrated her birthday with Aunt Tillie and Aunt Anna at a Chinese restaurant. When she arrived home her father sat at the kitchen table, a bottle of whiskey before him. He screamed obscenities at her. Calmly, Vicki picked up the bottle and crashed it down on his head. Blood spurted as he fell to the floor. Her aunts rushed into the apartment, saw what had happened, and took George to the hospital. Afterward Vicki cleaned up the whiskey, the broken glass, and her father's blood. Then she went to sleep.

The next morning Vicki was filled with remorse. She tried to shake off the feeling but when she saw her father's bandaged head she wept. George wept, too. Then Vicki embraced her father, and both asked for forgiveness.

Afterward, George promised to join AA. He stayed on the wagon until Vicki graduated high school. Then he went off the wagon. All through college and law school Vicki studied in the bedroom while George raged in the kitchen. When she graduated and was offered a position with the District Attorney's office because of her outstanding grades, Vicki moved out.

Her father never touched her after the incident on her sixteenth birthday, which taught Vicki an important lesson. After that she never let her guard down, especially with men.

Because of this experience Vicki dated infrequently. When she did, and a man tried to make love to her, she'd be furious.

Vito broke into her thoughts. "Let's get out of here before the place becomes completely chaotic," he suggested.

Vicki turned to him and took his arm. "Righto!"

They wove a path through reporters, courtroom observers, and friends and foes of John Hammer. Suddenly Vicki was pushed by an eager cameraman. She tripped. When she regained her balance the baby-blue eyes of the defendant stared at her.

"Bitch," he whispered under his breath.

Vicki's face shone with pleasure. Yes, she was a bitch—a bitch every man had to reckon with.

When Vicki arrived home she threw her jacket on the couch and tugged at her blouse. Something in her gesture was very prim, suggesting a fidgety schoolgirl chafing at the strictures of an overly rigid upbringing.

Vicki felt that there was a stranger inside of her, sometimes warring, sometimes calm, sometimes at odds with the rest of her personality—a stranger who had begun to come to the surface more often since her father's murder.

When George Giotti's body was discovered, Vito vowed to break the case.

"Vicki, the boss won't let you work with me," Vito said, "but don't worry. I'll assign every available investigator to find your father's murderer."

"I know who did it."

"Tucci?"

"It's obvious."

"His gun was found at the murder scene, but he reported it stolen a year ago. That's not enough hard evidence to bring him to trial."

"Why is he in hiding?"

"His disappearance could be about mob trouble and not have anything to do with your father's murder."

"He's the murderer," she said angrily, her face suddenly flushed.

Startled, Vito realized that Vicki was uncharacteristically out of control. As an attorney, Vicki always insisted on a cool, level-headed analysis of facts. It was one of the reasons she was so effective.

"It's impossible for you to be objective. After all, it is your father we're talking about. That's why the boss doesn't want you to work on this case," Vito said.

"He's not going to stop me," she retorted.

"You're going to jeopardize your entire career?

You'll look like an idiot." Then Vito softened his voice. "I know you loved your father. . . ."

"I hated him," she said vehemently. Realizing the effect of her words, she added, "I mean I had problems with him."

"You don't have to tell me about Italian fathers. Mine's a bitch. And he's tougher on my sister."

Vicki's face was a contradiction of expressions— part sadness, part confusion, part anger.

"When someone dies we only remember the good times, Vicki," Vito added gently.

"There were no good times," she said.

Vito put his arms around her. "There, there, Vicki. I'm your pal, right?" Silently she nodded her head. "Listen to me. Stay out of your father's investigation. You're too involved. You want to blame someone for his death. It'll make you feel better about the fact that you had a difficult time with him. But that's not what we do, is it? You're always talking about how cool-headed we have to be. You're right. This is one time when you can't be cool. This is one time when you're out of control."

When he looked into her lovely eyes he knew that his words fell on deaf ears.

"I'm going to take a long vacation," she said.

"Don't do it, Vicki," he warned. "The boss won't like it."

As hard as he'd tried, Vito couldn't stop her. She'd worked extra hours for so long that she had accrued lots of vacation time. Besides, she had another important reason for needing time off from her demanding job.

Her stomach felt tight, and she remembered the

doctor's advice about relaxing. She sat on the plush couch, slipped off her shoes, and put her feet up. Her apartment comforted her.

The duplex overlooked the Hudson River from its fifteenth-floor perch. On the first level was a ruby velvet couch opposite an electrically operated fireplace. On a metal table a stuffed pigeon faced a French art nouveau candelabra. Metal chairs placed about the room added to its sparsely furnished look.

The top level of the duplex was a bedroom/study with one major piece of furniture, a combination oak bed and bookcase with bracket shelves on each side. All of the windows in the duplex were uncovered, and the view of the skyline of New Jersey, across the river, looked like a painting.

She wanted a glass of wine. As she rose from the couch her blouse kept riding up. She decided to undress but first poured a glass of wine from the decanter on the sideboard. She climbed to the top level and opened the closet. A row of dark suits hung ready for her court appearances. She undressed and donned a burgundy robe.

She sat on the bed and looked out at the river. It was a lovely sight, and she loved the thought that she lived on an island. She turned and caught her reflection in a mirror.

Her fiery red hair and sparkling hazel eyes brightened the translucent paleness of her satiny skin. Everything about Vicki was delicate: her slim body, her fragile chin, her elegant nose, and her long, delicate fingers.

She prayed her baby would be gorgeous. She passed her hand over her womb and tapped a Morse code message of love to her child. Flushes of warmth filled her being at the thought of her precious baby, alive inside of her.

Feeling love frightened Vicki. She remembered a time when she was very young and someone had held her with incredible warmth and caring. She remembered that someone sang to her. She remembered sleeping without fear.

Whenever these memories surfaced Vicki was filled with an agonizing yearning for her mother.

But her mother was lost to her forever. And in her stead was her father's love, a frightening roller coaster of fury, remorse, and reconciliation.

Vicki knew that the emotional deprivation of her childhood affected her appearance. Vito described her as an Audrey Hepburn with red hair, for she looked like a delicate match girl. But the truth was that Vicki was all bitch and enjoyed the startled look in people's eyes when they saw her sharpness.

Her nostrils flared as she thought of Vito. She should have gone to dinner with him. But she didn't want her life complicated.

She had her future planned. She had paid Paul Johnson, a handsome and intelligent actor, to provide her with it.

"How do you want to make love?" Paul asked.

He was handsome, intelligent, courteous, and kind—qualities she wanted for her child.

"Is it in our contract?" she asked.

"Guess I'll have to be inventive. What do you like?"

She was ashamed to tell him she was a virgin.

"Let's pretend we're in love," Vicki suggested.

"Have some wine."

He poured a glass from the bottle he'd brought. He wanted to please Vicki, for she wanted a baby desperately.

Three glasses later Vicki was relaxed. When Paul's hand reached her thighs she didn't protest. His fingers touched her panties, then caressed her vaginal area. When he kissed her, her lips opened. Suddenly he was unbuttoning her blouse, kissing her neck, her breasts.

When he spoke his tone was soft and gentle. "Darling, I want you," he whispered.

Vicki sighed with pleasure.

The bra undone, his lips captured her nipples, and he fondled her with his tongue. Vicki struggled with her skirt as Paul stripped. When she saw his erect penis she had an urge to feel it. Hesitantly she touched him. He moaned as his fingers explored her. Then, gently, he entered her.

"You were a virgin," he said afterward. "I didn't know."

For a month she and Paul made love, and Vicki couldn't believe how much she enjoyed it. When her pregnancy was confirmed she was thrilled.

"Here's the balance of your fee, Paul. Thank you," she said to him.

"We can still see each other."

"I'm afraid not. I think it would be a mistake."

"Vicki, I care about you."

"That's not part of our bargain," she said, dismissing him, but not without regret.

She must have fallen asleep. She was awakened by the intercom. When she responded the doorman reminded her that her mail was in the lobby. Would she like it delivered to her door?

When the mail arrived she glanced through the pile. A blue envelope postmarked Peekskill, New York, captured her attention. The handwriting was beautiful. Vicki opened the envelope and read:

My darling daughter.

Her mind snapped to attention. Had her father written to her before he was murdered? But why was the letter postmarked Peekskill?

She read on:

We have not seen each other since you were two years old.

The letters blurred as tears filled her eyes. Could this be true? She wiped her eyes and focused on the amazing message. Quickly she reached the end:

I want you to know that I have always loved you. I still love you very much. Your Mother.

No. Someone has made a mistake, she thought, struggling to remain calm.

Maybe there was a connection to her father's death. She would go to the Convent of the Sacred Heart on Sunday to find out what this was about.

🍂 *Chapter 2* 🍂

A statuesque blonde in stiletto heels swiftly sauntered down SoHo's West Broadway. Her shiny black
dress looked as if it were made of plastic that had been
heated, then poured over every curve. Her large dark
glasses covered most of her face. The rest of it was
hidden behind her lion-mane hair.

She walked down the street as if she owned it due
to the fact that she had been born a few blocks away,
before SoHo was SoHo. Arianna Tucci had been an
infant in the mid-fifties when West Broadway was a
center of small industry where Italian, Hispanic, and
Chinese women toiled long hours. Whenever a factory
closed down, painters, sculptors, and dancers, needing large work spaces, rented the floors. By the mid-
sixties the Village artistic community had come to
dominate the area and renamed it SoHo.

In the eighties SoHo was crammed with boutiques,

galleries, restaurants, and other hallmarks of success. Many Italians still lived there. Most families were working-class, though a professional group was emerging.

Unfortunately, the most visible Italians were the illegal ones, like Arianna's father.

He was one of the reasons that when Arianna shopped, boutique owners quickly appeared.

The other reason was that Arianna was a rock star.

"Arianna, I have special things to show you," the jeweler, Jacques Perro, said as she passed his doorway.

"I need something very special for my concert," Arianna said warmly.

Jacques was a young man with ruddy cheeks and sultry eyes. "Come in," he beckoned.

The shop was modern and flashy. At one end an elegant woman was examining a black pearl and smiling her approval to the salesman. Arianna giggled because the woman sported a coiffure that looked like cotton candy.

Like Arianna's own wild mane, its aim was for effect.

On stage and off, rock stars were supposed to be wild, but Arianna yearned to appear in public devoid of this image. Couldn't she simply be Arianna, a normal woman, like a woman who shops at Bloomie's instead of SoHo boutiques? A woman who visits the public library instead of rehearsal halls? A woman who goes to the movies with a date, instead of cavorting in front of audiences in seminudity?

Arianna?

Who is she?

As if searching for an answer, Arianna scrutinized the designer jewelry in the case, for she shopped to invent new personas. Her search was obsessive, as was evident from her crammed closets.

Jacques pointed to a diamond necklace with black steel springs on yellow and white gold; an art deco diamond brooch trimmed with stones of deep blue-violet tanzanite; an onyx, lapis lazuli, and gold ring; and a diamond bracelet with black leather.

"Let me see the brooch," Arianna said.

The brooch's design was an elegant variation of the one worn by the woman in the faded photograph in her desk drawer—a likeness of her mother before she died.

"It is wonderful, isn't it?" Jacques whispered lovingly as he placed the brooch on a blue velvet pad. "Did you know that tanzanites were discovered only twenty years ago in Tanzania?"

Arianna smiled. One of the reasons she shopped in SoHo was that the shopkeepers were unusually knowledgeable.

"Who inspired the pin?" Arianna asked.

His eyes grew teary. "My mother loved art deco jewelry. Like you, I must be inspired by deep emotions before I create. You write songs from your heart. That's why the public loves you," he gushed.

Removing her large black glasses, Arianna examined the brooch closely.

"I love it." Gently, she squeezed his hand. "Thanks for sharing your memories with me," she said softly.

"Wear it at the concert and I will be happy," Jacques said.

"But the pin's beauty will be lost. I'm wearing an outrageous costume."

"Then wear it on an important personal occasion," Jacques suggested.

"I promise."

"Shall I send it around to your town house?"

"I'll take it."

"But it's valuable."

"Don't worry."

"Don't forget to insure it."

She smiled at him as he ceremoniously wrapped the package.

Nowadays Arianna charged purchases. When she was a rebellious teenager she had simply taken them.

Twenty years ago, when she was fifteen, the manager of a shop called her father because she had shoplifted. The police weren't informed because Mr. Tucci might be offended.

Tony Tucci walked into the chic shop, his ascetic face angry. As Tony's bodyguards watched the doorway the shop manager trembled, but not Arianna.

"I'm sorry for my daughter's prank," Tony said.

"She's young," the manager replied.

"What is the price of the bracelet?"

"Five hundred."

Quickly, Tony took a large wad of bills from his breast pocket, peeling out five, then another five.

"This is for your trouble," he said. "Come on, Arianna."

"No."

"I don't want to tell you a second time."

She shrugged, her curly hair framing her innocent

face. Her blue eyes blinked at her father's wrath, but she steeled her body. She walked outside and stepped into the waiting black Cadillac. When her father joined her he asked, "Why do you do these things? You know they pain me."

"I like to take risks. Like you do, Papa."

"Don't be like me. I want you to be a lawyer. Or a doctor."

"I can see New York University law school letting me enroll. The daughter of Tough Tony? Never," she said bitterly.

"If you want to go to New York University, I'll get you into New York University."

"No, thanks. Whatever I want in life I'll get on my own."

"You'll need me," he said grimly.

But she hadn't. Her singing career had taken off, despite her father's objections.

"Why do you want to work at a place like that?" he asked, referring to Le Club.

"I'm a star there, that's why."

"Arianna, I've tried to keep you out of the spotlight. It's dangerous for your picture to be in newspapers and on television."

"Dangerous for me or dangerous for you?"

"Don't be disrespectful," he cautioned.

"I can take care of myself."

He tried to protect Arianna by hiring bodyguards for her safety and for his peace of mind. But Arianna wanted to soak up as much life as she could, and show business was exciting. Like her father, she thrived on action.

When she was a child his activities existed in shadows. She learned about his secret life the hard way.

He insisted that she attend a private school and enrolled her in St. Margaret's, a Catholic grammar school where none of the girls liked her. At first she thought it was because she was Italian, since most of her schoolmates weren't. Later, when one threw a *Daily News* on her desk, Arianna realized it was her father's notoriety that kept her apart from the others.

"Your father is a gangster," the girl said, loud enough for the entire class to hear.

Arianna looked at the newspaper. There was a photograph of her father that identified him as a member of the Mafia. She went home and asked him about it.

"Darling, the newspapers are against Italian businessmen. That's why they say we are Mafia."

"What's Mafia?"

"It's an organization of people who protect Italians. Italians are always taken advantage of, so the Mafia was organized to help them fight back."

"What do they do?"

"They watch over us, like guardian angels."

She repeated this to the fancy girl in the fancy school, but the girl didn't believe Arianna. When Arianna was older she realized that her former schoolmate was right. By that time it didn't matter, though, because she wanted to be a singer, and a singer did not need an education. In high school she skipped classes to hang out with the rockers. When she came home too late her father punished her and would not let her out of the apartment.

Arianna waited. At seventeen she bolted. After she left home she tried to stop loving him.

When Jacques handed Arianna the beautifully wrapped package he said, "Wear it in good health."

Quickly, she left the shop. In public Arianna was usually conscious of her image, but today she did not want to be noticed or followed by fans. She strolled at a leisurely pace, but several passersby pointed to her. She quickened her pace as the form-fitting Karl Lagerfeld dress clung to her shapely body. She dug into her satchel for a crushed straw hat. Pulling it over her head, she tucked in the wisps of golden hair.

"Arianna!" a couple of fans shouted.

They ran up to her, blocking her path. The punks wore black leather and silver.

"Wow," said the first young girl.

"This is awesome," her friend said. Her hair was pink and blue and cut close to her head.

"I'm in a hurry," Arianna apologized, not wanting to insult her fans.

"Don't go yet," the first girl said. She was a tough type sporting an Apache haircut, yet her smile revealed that she was very young. "Are you writing new songs?" she asked. "I love your latest album."

"I can't wait for the concert," her friend said. "I hope it's not sold out."

"There are a few tickets left," Arianna said.

"Could I have your autograph?"

Arianna wrote her name, then said, "I must be going."

Swiftly, she left them. At MacDougal Street she ran up the steps of her town house. She looked up the street and spotted her father's men—her shadows—following her.

Inside she tossed her packages on the table in the narrow hall and walked into the large living room. The room was yellow and white, refreshingly accented with porcelain blue. Several brass-based glass cube end tables held architectural fragments, minerals, and crystals. Two oversized white couches stood on opposite sides of the room. Instead of cocktail tables, sculptural bronze pieces by Eigge were placed close to the couches. In one corner a white grand piano dominated, accentuated by three tall windows lined with bamboo plants. This alcove opened up into the dining room, which featured a long table and six chairs. Overhead a large skylight showered the area with sunshine.

"Martha?" Arianna called to her housekeeper, who might be upstairs in one of the bedrooms or possibly shopping. There was no answer as Arianna checked the writing desk for phone messages, hoping Robert had called. Nothing. Damn him!

Her concert was to take place in two weeks, and she had an enormous number of things to do. She needed new songs and was writing them with Jo Jo Johnston, her accompanist. Robert had been at rehearsals, constantly encouraging her new music, until page one exploded with the Tucci-Giotti situation.

After that, Robert disappeared. His office said he was out of town for a few days. She didn't understand his behavior. From the beginning of their relationship he had known she was the only child of Tough Tony Tucci, the head of one of the East Coast Mafia families.

Shrugging her shoulders, she checked the mail. A fat envelope from the clipping service. A bunch of fan mail. Books and magazines. The usual bulk mail from department stores.

She spied a handwritten letter. Everything was computerized these days, so the pale blue envelope commanded her attention. She picked it up and walked to the study at the rear of the house.

Setting a lovely mood was a small white fireplace with a Jasper Johns print above it. A throne chair of woven print fabric stood at the right, where mirrors were placed to widen the room. A wheat-colored wall-to-wall carpet was a somber background for the large brass pots filled with small trees. An old-fashioned rolltop oak desk was strewn with correspondence and publicity shots of Arianna that had to be signed.

Arianna kicked off her shoes and switched on the television set. Reporter Mary Adams was covering her father's story. Mary was out for blood, as was the victim's daughter, Vicki Giotti, an assistant district attorney. Everyone ignored the fact that George Giotti had intended to kill Tony. If her father was guilty, which Arianna doubted, he must have snapped.

When Tony's face flashed on the television screen Arianna quickly made the Sign Of The Cross.

"Please, God," she whispered, "my father is a sinner, but can You forgive him? He's been good to the poor. He's helped people in trouble. Please, please, protect him. If he's done this horrible thing, let the police find him and arrest him. Maybe he'll have a chance in court. Maybe they won't railroad him."

Fearfully, she prayed. Afterward she switched off

the set and opened the pale blue envelope, noting the Peekskill, New York postmark.

When she read the first words Arianna trembled:

My darling daughter.

What on earth? Why was her father writing to her?

She reached for the phone, but the next words stopped her.

We have not seen each other since you were a baby. I am sorry for that, but I have watched over you like a guardian angel, my darling Arianna. Your father probably told you that I was dead. I didn't approach you because I have always been afraid of him. Now I want you to know about me. I have given my photograph to Mother Teresa, who will send it to you when the time is right. I want you to know that I have always loved you. I still love you very much. Your Mother.

Her mother?

Arianna shivered. Was this a silly attempt at humor from a fan? She looked closely at the photograph. Her head began to pound. She jumped up and ran to the desk. From a drawer she took out her mother's photograph. Comparing the two, she realized there was a strong resemblance.

Could they be the same woman?

Had her father lied to her?

Hesitantly, she read the postscript, written in a different handwriting:

Can you come to the Convent of the Sacred Heart on Depew Road in Peekskill next Sunday at ten A.M.? Mother Teresa.

Could this be a media trap? Or perhaps the police were the authors of this scenario.

Well, Arianna thought, if they want a show, I'll give them a damn good one.

❧ *Chapter 3* ❧

*A*n exquisite garden surrounded the Convent of the Sacred Heart. A broad terrace flanked the main house, where a canopy of lavender blossoms led to a tall stone fountain on which birds perched to drink. The terrace sported stone boxes where rambler roses, blue hydrangeas, and pink and white snapdragons flourished. The sounds of nature, the rustle of shifting leaves, the chirping birds, and the soft rush of wind across the sky added to the peace and solitude of the convent.

On the terrace, seated at a large, round stone table, Arianna and Vicki waited impatiently while Mother Teresa poured tea.

Upon arrival each had been shocked at the other's presence. Trying to be polite, they couldn't help but notice each other's barely controlled fury.

The nun, observing them closely, saw they were a

study in contrasts. Vicki was pale, while Arianna's face was flushed with the pink blush from a bottle. Vicki wore the tart scent of British toilet water, but Arianna's French Opium had a stronger, spicy scent.

Arianna wore a dramatic black and white silk halter accessorized with freshwater pearl earrings, necklace, and rings. Vicki wore a Giorgio Armani suit with a crinkled white silk blouse. She accessorized her outfit with an antique silver necklace and bracelet.

Arianna's tawny blond hair was tossed like a lion's mane, a look that had become her trademark. Vicki wore her red hair pulled back in a soft roll that showed off her delicate, swanlike neck.

Mother Teresa's movements were quick and efficient as she poured tea from an antique silver teapot. On the table was a tray with an expandable toast rack filled with toasted wheat bread, a Victorian cheese board offering two types of cheese, ironstone plates, and silverware. The teacups and saucers were a lovely porcelain blue.

After the nun served each woman she waited as they sipped the tea in forced silence. She was a modest woman, never one to make too much of herself, though she had given up a career as a successful classical pianist. Now her fingers were in motion as they ran up and down the silver rosary that hung from her waist. Although she was seventy, Mother Teresa wore a short navy-blue skirt, short veil, and black low-heeled shoes. The outfit seemed perfect for her youthful exuberance, and her sparkling personality offset her age.

She leaned forward, speaking in a hushed tone of voice.

"A garden without a bench or table is like a room that isn't lived in," she said. "When I sit here it seems that all the world's cares are far away." She sipped her tea, then chuckled. "Of course, we all know that's not true."

"It is lovely," Vicki concurred nervously. She couldn't shake the feeling that something strange and awesome was about to happen.

"Gardening is a very civilized hobby. You can go anywhere in the world, phone a gardener up, and he or she will always be hospitable. Francesca Cella was our gardener."

"Who is Francesca Cella?" Arianna asked.

Mother Teresa's shoulders slumped forward conveying sadness. Her hands trembled as she picked up a pair of small dark glasses from the table. When she wore them they gave her a sophisticated look, though she conveyed a wholesome, maternal manner.

"Francesca lived and worked at the convent," she explained. "When I met her she had nowhere to go. She was despondent. Her life had been filled with hardship. She said that she was cursed. I don't believe that God does that to people. I tried to convince Francesca that she had choices in life, though she felt terribly trapped. I was overjoyed when she began to believe in God again."

"Why was she unhappy?" Vicki asked.

"Her children were taken from her. She was afraid to fight for them, though I feel the courts are on the mother's side. But Francesca felt that she had no choices in life . . . that men have all the power and there is no use fighting them. No one taught Francesca that she had rights. You see, things were very different thirty-five years ago.''

The women listened respectfully but were impatient to learn why they had been summoned to the convent.

"Mother Teresa, I respect you because you're a nun. But I'm shocked that you're part of this scam," Arianna said in a clipped tone of voice.

"What scam is that?" the nun asked.

"Why have you asked me to come here, and does it have anything to do with my father?"

"Not directly."

"Then you are involved." Arianna jumped up from her chair and searched nearby trees and flowerpots. "Are they hidden?" she demanded.

"What do I have hidden?"

"The cameras." Arianna tossed her long hair about as she confronted the nun.

"You are really crazy," Vicki said angrily.

"Listen, you're out to get my father, aren't you?" Arianna shouted.

"I work for the district attorney," Vicki answered, visibly upset. She turned toward the singer, her face beet red. "Your father is a killer."

"Look, bitch!" Arianna bit her lips. "I'm sorry, Mother. I didn't mean to curse."

Mother Teresa raised a hand in protest. "It's time to tell you why you're here," she said.

"Please do," Vicki said.

"I promised Francesca that I would bring both of you together when the time was right."

"Mother, don't be mysterious," Arianna said.

"I'm sorry. I don't mean to be mysterious," Mother Teresa said. "Before she left the convent Francesca left a gift for each of you. When I learned of the tragedy of your father's death," Mother Teresa said to Vicki, "I decided this was the right time to give Francesca's gifts to both of you."

"What does Francesca Cella have to do with my father?" Vicki asked.

"And why are we here?" Arianna echoed.

"Francesca Cella is your mother," Mother Teresa said.

There was a strained silence. Both women wore a pained expression coupled with a look of disbelief.

"What are you talking about?" Vicki whispered. "My mother is dead."

Inadvertently, Arianna nodded in agreement.

"It is very simple," Mother Teresa said softly. "Francesca Cella had two daughters with different husbands. And her gift to you"—she pointed to her two guests—"is each other."

She sucked in her breath sharply, then continued.

"You see, my dears, the two of you are *blood sisters*."

PART II

NEW YORK CITY

―――――1950―――――

FRANCESCA

🦋 Chapter 4 🦋

Bless me, Father, for I have sinned," Francesca Cella whispered.

Father Pietro looked through the confessional booth screen and recognized the sixteen-year-old daughter of the baker, Bruno Cella. A devoted churchgoer, Francesca went to confession weekly.

She was a beautiful young girl, with lush red hair worn in a long bob with a crown of pigtails on top. Her deep green eyes and pale skin resembled those of the Madonna. Because he heard her confession regularly, Father Pietro knew that Francesca was oblivious to her beauty and its effect.

But she enjoyed dressing in the latest fashion, though he knew her parents disapproved, for Matilda Cella also confessed to him. What was wrong with her white cotton blouse with a Peter Pan collar worn with a madras peasant skirt? God had blessed the girl with great beauty, which the priest hoped would not be a curse. In confession one penitent boy talked about Francesca, relating sins of lust and soiled trousers, though admitting that Francesca was unaware of his desire. The boy was attracted to her dreamy-eyed beauty but said that Francesca did not know how truly sexy she was. Father Pietro advised the boy that his sins were not Francesca's responsibility—a concept that fell on deaf ears.

"Father?" Francesca broke into the priest's thoughts.

"What are your sins?" he asked her.

"I'm angry at my father," she said.

"Why?"

"He won't admit that things are different in America. In Italy girls are chaperoned until they marry. When I tell him that here girls are allowed to go to dances and parties, he says they're bad girls."

"What does your mother say?"

"My mother says that I have to obey my father. She doesn't like to cross him. But I'm sixteen! They treat me like I'm a baby."

"Have patience," the priest said. "Say three Hail Marys and one Our Father. And be a good daughter, my child."

The priest shut the tiny door over the screen. On the other side Francesca felt frustrated. She needed to pour her heart out to the priest. In whom else could she confide?

Maybe I should tell him that I dream about my father's death, she thought. Ashamed, she made the sign of the cross.

Remembering it was Saturday afternoon, she left the

confessional hurriedly, for there was a long line of people waiting to go to confession, and she did not want anyone to think that she had many sins to confess.

Several women eyed her. Nervously, Francesca tucked in her blouse and walked down the church aisle.

The church was crowded because it was the day before St. Anthony's feast day. Tomorrow the festa would end ceremoniously with a procession.

St. Anthony's Church boasted fresco ceilings and stained glass windows. The center altar was crammed with rare silk cloths and real gold ornaments. Twelve marble pillars extending to the high ceiling had been transported from Italy stone by stone. Because of the church's opulence, St. Anthony's was called "the downtown cathedral," provoking pride among its working-class immigrant community.

Francesca knelt before the statue of St. Anthony in his brown friar's robe. She prayed, fingering her white pearl rosary beads—her First Holy Communion beads. Francesca loved their elegance. They were the only luxurious thing she owned. Quickly, she used the gold cross to make the Sign Of The Cross. Then she genuflected and headed for the church entrance, where women were selling blessed prayer books, medals, and church calendars to raise money for the church.

"Hello, Francesca," Mrs. Spella called. A widow with two sons, Mrs. Spella hoped Francesca would take a fancy to one of them. Shyly, Francesca nodded to her.

In front of the church several classmates gathered. Francesca envied Mary Murino's outfit—capri pants that stopped six inches above the ankle worn with narrow, low-cut black ballet shoes. Around her waist Mary wore a wide belt that gripped her ruffled blouse tightly, causing her bosom to swell. Though Mary wore a short "poodle" cut, her friend, Nancy Puna, teased her black hair into an elaborate bouffant. Nancy's eyes were rimmed with black liner, and her long lashes were covered with mascara. Both girls wore bright pink fingernail polish that matched their lipstick.

Her father called them tramps.

"Hi, St. Frances," Nancy called to her. The group around Nancy snickered at Francesca's nickname.

Francesca blushed. Quickly she walked away, but their laughter haunted her. She would give anything to be one of the crowd who went to movies and dances together. Instead she spent nights at home with her parents.

She turned up MacDougal Street and walked toward Washington Square Park. Then she sat on a park bench and watched a group of Italian men play *morra*, the game of throwing fingers. Her father was one of them.

It was a simple game. At a given signal each of two men shot a hand forward, extending one to five fingers. Simultaneously each man called out a number, guessing the total fingers extended by both. The one who was closest to the actual total won.

Alfredo Mayo waited for Bruno Cella to play, but Bruno delayed, hoping to see Alfredo's call. Several spectators shouted *"Mascalzone."* Bruno's face turned beet red at being called a scoundrel. He slammed his hand on the park railing and scraped his shoe soles on the curbstone as if erasing the entire matter. Formally he tipped his wide hat to the group and pointed two forefingers at them in a gesture resembling a goat's horns.

Angry murmurs surfaced among the men, for they recognized the familiar sign of the evil eye.

Undaunted, Bruno Cella placed his right hand on his left arm and bent the elbow, conveying the "screw you" gesture. Then he saw his daughter.

"What are you doing here?" he demanded.

Francesca cringed. Why did her father act like an animal? Work. Eat. Sleep. That was his life. The Italian way.

But she was an American girl and wanted to escape this claustrophobic neighborhood where life was viewed only in her father's terms.

Francesca knew there was a different world. A world where people spoke beautifully. A world where everyone was well dressed. A world where men were gentle. A world where women were happy.

The next day was sunny, drawing crowds for the festa's final event. People stood on the church steps watching a band of musicians wearing green and yellow costumes and tall hats with feathers walk up the street. Several young boys followed the musicians, taunting them. Behind the boys were worshippers—older women wearing long black skirts and blouses, their hair bound tightly around their heads; younger mothers grasping children by the hand; giggling girls walking arm in arm.

At the rear of the procession eight strong men carried a platform bearing a statue of St. Anthony. The statue was covered with a long white robe elaborately trimmed in gold; hundred-dollar bills were pinned on it.

The procession moved slowly because Sullivan Street was narrow. Pushcarts selling religious objects, Italian cakes and candies, zeppoli, and calzones lined the street. One pushcart offered spicy foods, and a ruddy-faced man slapped veal parmigiana into large loaves of fresh bread for hungry customers.

When the procession reached the church the musicians picked up their horns to blast "Santa Lucia." As they climbed the stairs sweat from the hot June sun dripped off their faces. People scrambled to get into church before the procession so the best seats wouldn't be taken.

Inside the church old women fondled statues and prayed fervently as a younger group whispered about the dance scheduled for eight P.M. When the statue of St. Anthony was placed at the altar Father Mike appeared with two altar boys, and the service began.

In the rear of the church thirty-year-old George Giotti, dressed in his New York City policeman's uniform, intently scanned the worshippers. A few pews away he spotted his sisters. Tillie's bouffant hairdo and long earrings were hard to miss. Beside her, Anna wore her hair in a braid twist, a somber contrast to her sister.

He signaled them that he was leaving. His job was done. He had examined the faces in church and knew that the Black Hand was not present.

"You're a natural, Georgie Porgie," his captain, Michael Lafferty, had said earlier at the precinct. "You're a dago, And dagos talk to other dagos."

"My family moved out of that neighborhood twenty years ago. I haven't too many ties."

"Sniff around. See what you can find out."

George walked down the steps, recognizing familiar faces. Some said hello.

"Hello, George. How are your sisters?" one woman asked.

"They're in church." Politely, George tipped his hat at the woman.

'He passed the sausage shop and the ricotta store, where the aroma of spices filled his nostrils. His stomach felt queasy because of last night's whiskey. His sisters complained about his lack of appetite. Fasting will keep me trim and slim, he thought as he spied his reflection in a window. He had not gained an ounce since he'd played ball at St. Francis of Assisi on Sixteenth Street.

George was proud of his military appearance. His figure was lean and taut. His sharp nose dominated his face, conveying an expression of authority. His black eyes were deep and intense. His once-curly hair, now cropped close to his head, was hidden under his policeman's hat.

George walked up Houston Street, turning on Sixth Avenue. In the center of the block was a private social club for Italians. Two black Cadillacs were parked outside. In the drivers' seats were muscular men. That meant the Black Hand was here.

George spotted a coffee shop across the street and went in. Sitting at a table by the window, he sipped coffee while watching the club. All was quiet, so he filled his time watching other passersby.

The area was the thoroughfare not only for the

Italian community but also for the bohemian group of artists and rebels. Two men in long, flowing capes sauntered by, discussing politics with another man, probably a painter, dressed in dungarees and a plaid shirt.

George spotted a group of greasers who slouched in skin-tight black jeans, black boots, and black leather motorcycle jackets. The boys sported long hair styled into a greasy duck's tail. The girls wore short leather skirts, hot-pink tights, and shaggy haircuts.

Two Italian women sat on a stoop staring at the tough group. Sensing disapproval, a greaser made obscene gestures at the women. His pals grabbed him, hurried to the corner, and crossed the street.

Suddenly five men exited a neighborhood bar. All carried baseball bats. The greasers scrambled. Two were caught and had their heads pounded methodically. Watching the blood flow, other greasers went to their buddies' aid but were caught up in the brutal onslaught. They screamed obscenities at the attackers, further igniting the violence. Finally someone called to the Italians from inside the bar. Hesitantly they stopped the attack, disappearing inside the confines of the bar.

The greasers stumbled down the street. No one took any notice.

George came to attention as two men exited the private club. One of them was Tough Tony Tucci, an ambitious young mafioso. Tony checked the street, then nodded to his cohort, who disappeared inside the club.

Surrounded by three men, Don Guido Allegro appeared. Tony ushered the don swiftly into the second car. Then he hopped into the first car. The cars drove away quickly.

Hurriedly, George paid for his coffee and left the shop, running up the street to see in which direction the cars were headed. When he turned the corner he collided with a young woman.

"Ohhhhhhhh," she whimpered.

"I'm sorry," George said. "Have I hurt you?"

"You've hurt my ankle," Francesca Cella murmured.

George looked into the face of the most beautiful girl he had ever seen. His heart beat so rapidly, he felt like a fool.

"Can you walk?" he asked.

"Not really," she complained.

"Where do you live?"

"My father's bakery is down the block."

"Then I will have to carry you," George said as he gallantly swung Francesca's young body up into his arms and carried her down the street.

☘ *Chapter 5* ☘

*B*runo Cella worked with a ready smile on his face.

"Ciao," he called to his customers as they pointed to the loaf of bread they wanted. He laughed gustily as he wrapped the freshly baked bread into the crisp white paper, tying it with red string that he broke on the knuckle of the third finger of his left hand. Then he said something nice about the customer's family.

"Your son is handsome."

"Your baby is beautiful."

These niceties kept Bruno's world revolving and presented him as good-natured and sunny in disposition. Yet most of the neighborhood men knew Bruno as a man of *sangue freddo,* "cold blood." His history qualified him for this description; in Italy, Bruno had worn the brown shirt of the fascists. And Bruno's courtship of Matilda Corso employed the fascistic virtues of brutality and abuse.

He was traveling through Calabria when he spotted the lovely young girl.

"Is she promised?" he asked an old man in the square. The man replied that Matilda was in love with a young man from a neighboring town, but the banns had not been announced in church.

Early the following morning Bruno waylaid the young woman. When she protested his advances, he told her he would kill her if she didn't marry him. Terrified, Matilda promised her love forever.

Matilda's father was dead, and she had no brothers. Her mother and she did not dare disobey a man with the strong passions Bruno displayed.

She became his faithful and devoted wife, obedient, silent, and passionless. When she gave birth to his daughter her husband mourned.

"I want a son," he complained.

"I do everything wrong," she admitted.

"You're no good. You've never been any good. You will never be any good," he said, repeating his familiar litany.

Matilda cowered under his fury. But with the birth of her beautiful daughter she had one pleasure in life: her daughter, Francesca.

As Francesca flowered Bruno kept the reins tight, so Matilda dutifully accompanied her daughter everywhere. She knew that Bruno was looking for the right man to take Francesca off their hands. When George Giotti began courting her daughter, Matilda prayed to the Madonna to shower happiness on the young girl. But the Madonna chose to ignore Matilda's prayers, because Bruno arranged for their daughter's marriage with the same brutality he had used to arrange his own.

"But Papa, I don't really know him. How can I marry him?" Francesca protested.

"The wedding is arranged. That is that!"

"I'm in school. I want to get a good job when I graduate. If my marks are good, I can go to college. Papa, I want to go to college."

"College!" He banged his empty wineglass on the table. Immediately Matilda jumped to refill it, but he waved her away. At lunch he was a prudent drinker.

"Tell your daughter, Mama. Do women go to college? Go on, tell her."

"It's true, Francesca. Women don't need to go to college."

"This isn't Italy."

"No, this is America!" Bruno raised his fist in anger. "See this?" He pointed to a newspaper lying on the table. "Mother of two gets raped. Is that what you want? You want to go to college? You want to meet American men, these kind of men. You don't know what the world is like. Count your lucky stars, Francesca, that you have a good Italian man who wants to marry you and take care of you. Remember, he's a policeman, so no one will ever harm you."

"Other girls go to college, and nothing happens to them."

"*Putanas!* That's what they are. A good woman stays at home and takes care of her children."

"But—"

"Enough. You will obey me as long as you live under my roof."

Terrified of his anger, Francesca retreated into the safe haven of the bathroom.

She wept for a long time. Then she dried her tears and tried to think of an escape.

What could she do? For a moment she considered running away from home. She could get a job and live with other girls. That's what happened in the movies. She'd work and study and make a success of her life. Then she would marry someone she loved, instead of someone chosen by her father.

But how could she leave? What kind of work would she do? Be a shop girl? Perhaps. What if her father found her? She was legally underage.

She could refuse to marry George. And her father would throw her out of her home. Where would she go? She had no one.

She could hear her father's torments. "Who do you think you are?"

Who was she?

She wasn't like the other neighborhood girls. Her mother said she was different. She said that Francesca acted like a movie star. It was true that she went to the movies and studied Elizabeth Taylor. She copied Elizabeth's hairstyle, and her mother copied the star's clothes at the sewing machine. But Matilda refused to tighten the bodices so Francesca's slim waist could look like Elizabeth's.

Confused, Francesca put her head in her hands.

There was a soft knock on the bathroom door. "Francesca," her mother called. "Let me in."

Francesca opened the door.

"Your father went to the bakery," her mother said.

She sat on the bathtub edge, looking grim. "George seems like a nice man. Don't you like him?"

"He's okay."

"What else do you expect?"

"I don't know."

"Don't you feel anything? I mean—has he kissed you?"

"What am I supposed to feel?"

Her mother drew back, and her eyes looked blank.

"Wait until you're married. You'll love your husband, and you'll have babies." Matilda tucked in several curls that were escaping Francesca's barrettes. Then she kissed her daughter's forehead.

"George will be here soon. Get ready."

She left the bathroom. When she heard the lock click behind her she wondered why Francesca spent so much time there.

Behind the closed door Francesca examined herself in the bathroom mirror. The mirror hung over the bathroom sink, so she stood on the bathtub ridge to see herself.

She wore a swing skirt of navy-blue gabardine and a petticoat trimmed with eyelet that floated down to her ankles. Her blouse was white eyelet and featured a high neck and long sleeves. Underneath she wore a Maidenform bra that hurt her shoulder blades. If she loosened the straps, her breasts moved when she walked, which upset her mother. Although Francesca was slim, Matilda insisted that she wear a panty girdle so that no part of her body would be soft. Under the petticoat Francesca wore black stockings held up by garters on her panty girdle. Her shoes were flats.

Bruno said she couldn't wear heels or makeup until she married. Fortunately, her natural complexion produced a lovely blush, and her green eyes sparkled naturally.

The doorbell rang. Francesca jumped down from the bathtub and unlocked the door. In the kitchen she picked up her purse and kissed her mother goodbye.

"Your father said to be home at nine-thirty," Matilda warned.

"I will," Francesca promised, and she ran downstairs to meet George.

He took her to a Saturday matinee movie. Then they dined in a small Italian restaurant where he held her hand and told her how pretty she was. Francesca tried to talk to George about school and her dreams for the future, but he wasn't interested. Instead he complimented her on her outfit, her hair, her eyes, and her lips.

When they returned home it was eight forty-five. The entrance door was open, so they walked into the hall without ringing the Cella doorbell. Then George pulled Francesca under the stairs.

"What are you—"

"Shhh," he said. "No one can see us here."

George pressed his body close to her, causing her Maidenform bra to cup her breasts firmly. He whispered "I love you" as his penis pressed against her thighs. Her breasts swelled against his chest as his erection grew hard. He breathed heavily in her ears as he rubbed his body back and forth.

Francesca's body grew hot against him. He took her hand and placed it on his fly. His erection felt large as he covered her hand with his own. Then he went out of control. She wanted to move away, but he pinned her against the wall as he moaned into her ears.

"Oh, baby," he sighed as his penis went flat under her hand.

She thought about her father in the apartment two flights up. What would he do if he knew she was touching George Giotti's penis without benefit of marriage?

George was almost too handsome. His dark eyes shone in the dim light. His lips curled in an impulsive manner, and his smile conveyed a roguish style that sent shivers through her. Out of uniform George wore an expensive gray suit and matching fedora hat—an outfit that gave him a movie star aura.

Boldly, Francesca took George's hand and put it under her petticoat. Surprised, he kissed her. His mouth opened wide, and his tongue touched hers. She clung to him, feeling wet and shaky, and wondered if he put his mouth on her breasts would the aching stop. Slowly he unbuttoned her blouse and unfastened her bra. Then he took her breasts from the bra and with the tips of his fingers touched them, causing her nipples to swell. She felt that she would burst soon. He bent, his dark hair brushing her chin as he took one nipple in his mouth and sucked it. She felt helpless and pressed her body closer, as if he was the source of everything she needed. Then he put his mouth on the other nipple, sucking it so frantically that she tightened her arms around his neck.

His fingers tugged at the rim of her panty girdle, which did not give.

"Can you take that damned thing off?"

She pulled the girdle down quickly and stepped out of her shoes and stockings.

"That's better," he moaned.

His caressing fingers in her vaginal area caused her an uncontrollable yearning for him.

"My girl," he moaned. His fingers quickened as they found her opening. Gently, he put his finger inside to explore her.

"Do you know what belongs there?" he whispered.

"No."

"I belong there."

She knew he meant his penis and wondered how his big thing could fit into her small place.

"Want me to show you?"

She wanted to say yes, but something warned her to stop him. She knew too many stories about girls getting pregnant.

"It's wrong," she said.

"You're my girl, aren't you?"

She was silent, and his fingers stopped exploring down there.

"We're going to be married, Francesca," he said firmly.

"I'm only sixteen, and—"

"Your father agrees. Don't worry. I'll teach you everything you need to know."

"Can't we be engaged until I graduate?"

"I can't wait that long," he moaned.

Suddenly his fingers moved, and she was filled with an enormous aching feeling. Her body heaved as he touched her insides, and her head pounded furiously. She squeezed her body against him in a frantic motion.

"Want me to stop?" he teased.

"No," she pleaded.

"You like it, don't you? That's good. Baby, we'll do this every night. I'll touch you, and you'll touch me, and we'll feel like this. . . ."

Something began inside of her. Frightened, she grabbed him.

"Don't be scared, just let go," he whispered.

"But—"

"Just go with it. Go on, honey."

She closed her eyes tightly and let the wildness take over. She shook as he touched her secret places. She wanted something there and pushed forward, trying to fill her convulsive need. With his free hand George opened the zipper of his trousers, took her hand, and put it on his penis. She felt him grow hard against her fingers as he showed her how to rub it.

"Keep it up. Don't stop," he warned.

He began pumping his penis into her hand, using her as a funnel, the abrasive movements sending him wild.

"I'm going to . . ." he moaned.

Suddenly she lost herself. She held on to his pulsing organ as her body exploded. Her head pounded and her breath grew fast. In a series of passionate convulsions she became hot, wet, warm, and soft.

"Oh, baby. I want you so," George said.

She wanted him inside of her, wanted to lie against him, warmed by his body. She wanted to take care of him. Was this love? she wondered. He seemed helpless in her arms, as if she could give him everything he needed. Suddenly she felt very necessary to him.

"I'm dying to be inside you," he moaned.

Then he exploded. They held on to each other until

he quieted. Afterward he kissed her sweetly as he helped pull up her panty girdle and smooth her stockings. Then he tucked his penis back into his trousers.

"Kiss it for good luck," he said.

She bent to kiss him there. When she looked into his eyes they were filled with a startling gratitude and warmth that seemed like the answer to all her needs.

God bless America, Francesca thought, as she stood at the altar. Beside her, looking terribly handsome, George was nervous. She took his hand in hers. His fingers were cold, but when she touched him a soft smile appeared on his face. He looked at her, his dark black eyes sending messages of love.

In the first pew her parents gleamed with pride. George's parents were deceased, but his two sisters attended with their husbands. Several neighbors, sitting in the pews behind the families, beamed their approval.

Everyone is happy for us, Francesca thought. And she, too, felt a kind of happiness. But she was tormented by sadness for the future that would never be hers. She would never go to college. She could never be an American girl.

That's okay, she thought. I'll be happy with George. We'll love each other and have babies, and then I'll go back to school.

George wouldn't mind. George loved her. Didn't that mean that he would give her anything she needed?

❧ *Chapter 6* ❧

*O*h, it's impossible," Francesca moaned as she examined the patterned wall covering on the living room
walls of her Hudson Street tenement apartment. The
pattern was a free form in beige with a green design.
Against it the wing chair, the Castro convertible, and
the Philco television set looked shabby. The ornate
new lamps and gilded coffee table that were wedding
presents did nothing for the room either. Francesca
placed three colorful ceramic ashtrays around the
room. She had bought them in a small craft shop on
Eighth Street.

Last Saturday she had found a living room set she
adored.

"Oh, look, George," she exclaimed.

In the window of a furniture shop was a couch with
button tufting. Two small chairs matched the couch,

and the display also featured a kidney-shaped oak coffee table.

"It's our living room furniture," she said. "Do you like it?"

"It's a little offbeat," George remarked.

"You're always saying that you want to be an American," she responded. "This is really modern stuff. No one in the neighborhood has it."

He thought for a moment.

"Okay. But only if we can afford it."

Happily, she led him into the store. An hour later they exited with a contract for monthly payments on the set.

That night Francesca was especially loving.

George loved sex and wanted it all the time, but when she had her period she refused him. On those nights he was grouchy, left her alone, and drank too much at the Hudson Street Tavern across the street.

Now she sat at the kitchen table nibbling at a sandwich. The table and chairs were wrought iron, another modern touch in their home.

She looked through her old schoolbooks. She missed learning about new things and asked George if she could finish high school so she could get a diploma. But he said she was his wife and no longer a schoolgirl.

"Francesca, are you there?" Her sister-in-law, Tillie had a shrill voice.

Francesca smoothed her skirt and shirt quickly before she opened the door. Tillie's hairdo seemed even wider than usual.

"Want to come to Macy's?" Tillie's open smile seemed inviting, but Francesca knew better.

"I'm doing housework."

"I see." Tillie's eyes swept over the room. "You know," she said, "your father didn't give you very much when you married. We thought he'd furnish the apartment. But George has to pay for all this stuff."

She showed her disdain for the apartment's modernism by the tilt of her sharp nose.

"George doesn't mind," Francesca retorted.

"Well, bye," Tillie said, her dark eyes snapping.

Francesca closed the door with relief. Her sisters-in-law lived next door. In apartment 5C Tillie and her fireman husband, Larry Mella, argued most of the time. In apartment 5B Anna and her husband, Bob Commo, were quieter. Both sisters spied on Francesca.

Francesca felt like a prisoner. Her husband was fussy about the people she spoke to. "Don't talk to Nancy Puna," he said, learning that Francesca had casually spoken to her former schoolmate.

"Why?"

"She's no good. She's sleeping with her boyfriend."

Francesca did not remind George that before their marriage they had indulged in heavy petting. Now that they were man and wife George was stern in his sexual views.

"No, we won't go see that movie," he said when she asked about seeing *A Place in the Sun*.

"Why not?"

"There's too much indecent stuff going on."

"Like we do?" she teased.

His face turned beet red.

"Don't ever talk like that."

"Like what?"

"Like a tramp," he said.

She flinched at the word. Was George like her father?

Each day she walked down Bleecker Street and stopped at the bakery. Bruno was always busy, but he had a brief word for his daughter.

"See your mother?" he asked.

"I'm going there now."

"Good."

She waited for him to say something nice about her dress, her hair, anything. Now that she was a proper wife she expected her father to be nicer to her. But he wasn't.

She lunched with Matilda, who prepared delicate dishes of pasta and fagioli, frittatas, veal piccata, which she gave Francesca to take home.

"Heat this for supper. George will never know."

Unfortunately, Francesca let it slip, and George created quite a fuss.

"Why aren't you cooking? What do you do all day?" he demanded.

"But you don't have a big appetite. And it takes so long to cook for two people."

"Cook," he ordered.

She obeyed her husband. Right now a chicken was roasting in the oven.

When dinnertime arrived George did not appear. She waited for an hour. Then two. He finally arrived at eight o'clock with whiskey on his breath.

"Hi, baby." He slurred his words. "Let's fuck!"

He pinched her breasts so they hurt.

"Have something to eat first," she suggested.

"I want to eat you," he said.

He grabbed her harshly and pushed her into the bedroom. Quickly he stripped off her clothes. When he kissed her his breath smelled awful, and she turned her head away.

"Hey, don't do that," he said nastily.

Clumsily, he yanked off his uniform. She tried to fold it neatly, but he grabbed her and pushed her head onto his erect penis.

"Eat me," he said.

She clenched her teeth.

"I said eat me."

She wouldn't.

He slapped her face, and she burst into tears. But he didn't notice. He pushed her face down so hard that her bruised lips hurt when she opened her mouth.

"Watch your teeth," he said.

She opened her mouth wide, trying not to hurt him so that he wouldn't hit her again.

Harshly, he rammed his penis into her mouth. She felt as if she would suffocate if he didn't stop. Her throat constricted, and she needed to breathe. She panicked.

"Bitch!" he said as she pushed him away.

"George. Please."

"You don't like to give head?"

Again he forced her mouth open. She was crying, but still he didn't notice. He pushed his erection into her and pumped away. Then he moaned as his semen erupted into her unwilling orifice.

In the morning he was tender and apologetic.

"I think I got loaded last night," he said.

"George, did something happen? I mean . . ."

His face grew tense.

"Yeah, they passed over me at the precinct when I asked for night duty. I can make more money on that tour. And I could spend days with you. Wouldn't that be great?"

"But you would be sleeping."

"Not alone." He grinned. "Besides, I don't like you going out alone during the day."

"But I visit my mother."

"There's lots of guys hanging around. You're so pretty," he said, kissing her cheek. "Hey, what happened to your lip?"

"Don't you remember?"

"It looks like an infection."

She decided it would be better not to tell him that he had caused the bruises.

"So you're still working days?" she asked innocently.

He looked at her suspiciously.

"For now," he said.

"Come on, let's have breakfast. You'll be late for work."

"Naw. I'm taking the day off. I'm going to call in sick."

"What for?"

"To teach them a lesson."

She rose from bed and wrapped a robe around her naked body.

"Don't do that," George commanded from the bed.

"I have to make breakfast."

"Come back here," he said.

After that day Francesca's married life changed. Each night, as she waited for him, George drank with his buddies at the bar across the street. When he arrived home the same routine began.

First he pinched her breasts so they hurt. Then he led her into the bedroom, demanding that she perform sexually. If she performed well, George kissed her with his breath smelling of whiskey. Then he jammed his penis into her and one, two, three, he came.

To forget her humiliation she took daily walks through the Village and wondered if every wife had secrets. She spoke to her mother, but Matilda refused to listen.

"Obey your husband," she said.

"When George drinks he treats me like a whore."

"That's private. Don't tell me."

Francesca needed someone to talk to, someone she could trust. In the park she met an American girl named Jamie who lived on MacDougal Street. Often they exchanged the pleasantries of the day, but Francesca would not speak about anything personal to a stranger.

When she missed several periods Francesca did not tell George. Instead she blurted out the news to Matilda, who arranged for an appointment with the family doctor. During the examination Matilda remained in the room.

"I think you're pregnant. We'll do a test to be sure," the doctor said.

Francesca burst into tears, embarrassing Matilda.

"What's wrong, Francesca?" the doctor asked. "This should make you happy."

"I don't know if George will like it."

"Of course he'll like it. What man wouldn't want a child?"

Francesca threw a fearful look at her mother, but Matilda shrugged her shoulders in resignation. Francesca desperately wished she had a sister to talk to. She vowed if she had this baby, it would not be an only child. She would have many children so that they could have each other.

🍃 Chapter 7 🍃

*N*ineteen-year-old Jamie Jamison was young and restless. Her hair, dyed ink black, was cut short and sassy with a duck tail and greased. Her skin-tight black jeans, black hobnail boots, tight black T-shirt, and black leather motorcycle jacket were complemented by slanty black glasses trimmed with gold.

When she changed her address from Park Avenue to Greenwich Village Jamie destroyed her shirtwaist dresses, girdles, tight bras, lizard-skin handbags, and narrow stiletto shoes. She kept the white cashmere polo coat with its matching poodle cloth wizard cap to wear whenever she returned to her parents' home.

Her only other keepsake was her diamond wedding band.

It was an old-fashioned setting, an obvious choice for Charles Prescott III, who wore blue cotton broadcloth shirts with button-down collars and button cuffs, trim ties with stripes and small knots, black leather shoes tapered at the toe, gray flannel suits, single-breasted, straight-lined tweed overcoats and crew-cut hair. In summer Charles sneered at synthetic seersucker and wore Brooks Brothers' linen, though it wrinkled and was hot.

When she filed for divorce against Charles's wishes he hired detectives to follow her, though she wasn't asking for alimony. Charles couldn't believe that Jamie was not interested in his money.

She was dining at the family apartment, where pot roast and badly burned potatoes were served elegantly. By the time the overly sweet crème caramel came, Jamie was anxious to leave.

"Jamie, dear, you've had your fun. You've been living in that awful Village place for three months. Isn't it time you returned home?" her mother said.

Jamie shook her head violently.

"I want to live my own life. Grandmother Fowler left me a trust. I can live on that and earn money on my own."

Her mother glared.

"Are you insane, Jamie? You have a wonderful husband who adores you. How can you do this?"

"How do you merit Charles as wonderful? Oh, he's wealthy. And after he's done with Yale he'll join his father's firm and earn six figures for the rest of his life. He'll buy Old Greenwich property, and the most exciting thing in his life will be a new boat."

"What's wrong with that?" her father asked angrily.

"Nothing," Jamie said, her pink lipstick smearing her teeth as she gulped the last of her dessert.

"So?" Her mother waited.

"Charles is awful," Jamie said, tucking the tails of her black silk shirt into her tight jeans. "He doesn't know how to make love. He doesn't talk. He's an idiot. I'm not spending my life with him."

"You're insane." Her mother glared at Jamie, then turned to her husband. "Darling, we should have our daughter committed. She needs help."

"That maneuver is passé, Mother dear," Jamie retorted. "You can't get away with it in the fifties." Feeling her anger grow, she continued. "That's what our sort does to keep women in line if they won't obey the rules. Feminists blame men, but men don't have to lift a finger, do they, Mother dear?"

Jamie ground her teeth deliberately, knowing the sound would hit home. Her mother flinched as if she had been hit by a bullet. "No, siree, Mommeee. Not this time. You leave me alone or we'll have a nice scandal on our hands. I know all about the family skeletons. I'll talk to the *New York Times*. Would you like the Jamison family on page one? Hmmmm?"

Jamie took a Lucky Strike from a pack, lit it, and threw the match onto the dessert plate. Mrs. Jamison jumped up from her chair, ran to Jamie, took the match from the plate, and held it in a graceful pose until Alice, the maid, took it from her. Mrs. Jamison thanked the maid with a slight nod.

"So, Mom and Dad, you let me live my life, and I'll let you live yours," Jamie sneered. She saluted them in a military style, went out into the foyer, picked up her poodle coat and hat, and left. Once outside she hailed a cab and told the driver to take her to the Village Café at MacDougal and Bleecker streets.

When Jamie arrived she walked into the place, immediately feeling a change of mood.

The café bar was exciting. During the day it was frequented by Italians, but at night it became a meeting place for lefties, artists, bohemians, poets, and hangers-on from uptown like Jamie.

Many advertising and television people liked to mix with the downtown creative scene.

Chet Halstead was one of them. He was an old family friend who encouraged Jamie to free-lance for his agency, Halstead, Ltd. His firm created ads that sold Ritz crackers, Campbell's soup and Maidenform bras.

She spotted Chet at a table, drinking cheap red wine in a tall water glass because it was avant-garde. When he saw Jamie he smiled at her.

"How was Mom and Pop?" Chet asked when she joined him.

His freckle-faced-boy-wonder look was enhanced by a shock of bright red hair worn in a crew cut. He took off his tie and put it in his pocket to be more informal as he pawed a very blond chap with blue-green eyes.

"The same pitch," Jamie said. She looked over the crowd. "Cognac," she called to the short, squat waiter who knew her.

"Anyone here?" she asked Chet.

"I'm set for my evening," Chet whispered into Jamie's ear. "Isn't he gorgeous?"

"I thought you liked black boys."

"I'm democratic." Chet laughed as he lit a cigarette, inhaled it, and choked.

The waiter brought the cognac in a cheap shot glass. Jamie drank it down quickly.

"No one's here," she complained. "I like this place better in the afternoon."

"Is this where you spend your days?" Chet asked.

"Nighty night," she answered, and she left the bar.

The next morning Jamie wrote advertising copy for a soup ad that was a testament to the American family. At the center of her pitch was a perfect mother. At two P.M. a Halstead messenger picked up the copy.

Afterward Jamie lunched at the Village Café on martinis, veal, and peppers, then strolled down to Houston Street to visit St. Anthony's Church. Jamie sat in the quiet church watching the old Italian women, their harsh lives written on their faces as they privately spoke to the Lord. The passion on their faces moved her. It was quite different from the Anglicized Catholicism worshipped by her family.

She whispered a private prayer.

"Lord, please help me to find what I'm searching for. I don't know what it is. But I know what I have isn't enough. I want . . ."

Her throat felt dry, so she bent her head in silent prayer.

After church she shopped in the cheese store where women gossiped. Then she went to a coffee shop frequented by the locals. Afterward she walked up to Washington Square Park to watch the young children play.

She spotted Francesca sitting on a bench, looking pensive, so she didn't intrude on her privacy.

Francesca had everything—beauty, brains, and a warm heart—but she was afraid of life.

Not like Jamie, who insisted on greeting life with open arms.

Chapter 8

*M*ay I sit next to you?"

Startled, Francesca looked into two deep blue eyes. Neighboring park benches were unoccupied, so why did this man want to sit next to her? She smoothed her hair needlessly, hoping that her wedding band glinted in the sun.

She nodded her head but moved when he sat beside her. People strolled by. Courting couples. Bearded bohemians. A few drunks. The man glanced sharply at a group of Italian women who were staring at him.

Nausea overwhelmed Francesca. Embarrassed, she put her handkerchief over her mouth.

"Do you feel ill?" the stranger asked, handing her an elegant linen handkerchief.

"Oh, it's too beautiful!" she exclaimed.

"It's to use, not to admire," he said gently.

She wiped her mouth, inhaled the crisp air, and

hoped that the sickness that usually occurred at tea-time would pass. The doctor said this phase would be over soon. Francesca ate sparingly but felt very unattractive. Her mother said most women felt that way.

The week before they had shopped for maternity clothes to cheer up Francesca. Francesca found most maternity wear unattractive, so Matilda made outfits for her seventeen-year-old daughter to wear.

Francesca wore a navy blue two-piece set that her mother made. The top was large so that Francesca could grow into it. George hated the new clothes and insisted she wear her old ones when he was around, though they were tight and uncomfortable.

"You seem pensive," the man said.

"I don't know you."

"I'm Tony Tucci. I buy bread from your father's shop every day."

"Your wife has good taste."

"I have no wife." His eyebrows rose in a flirtatious manner.

Francesca lowered her gaze, first noting the shark-skin suit, the dark silk shirt, and the wonderful polka-dot tie. His shoes were pointed, a style she guessed was Italian. On his pinky finger he wore a large blue sapphire.

She wondered who he was. Then she remembered George complaining about a Tony Tucci, a gangster George wanted to arrest.

"You're George Giotti's wife. He's a very lucky man. When did you marry him?" Tony Tucci asked.

"A few months ago."

"I've been away. When I left, you were Bruno

Cella's little girl. And now you're going to be a young mother."

"Were you far away?"

"Italy. There was business to attend to."

"What business are you in, Mr. Tucci?"

"Olive oil. Tomato paste. Products from the old country."

"Do you like Italy?"

"Yes. In New York there is too much trouble and violence, too much going on."

"I love America," she said earnestly.

"The promised land. The American dream. Have your dreams come true?"

She avoided his question. "Were you born here?" she asked.

"I arrived when I was a child. I remember how it was on the boat. We were packed in like animals. When we docked the authorities treated us badly. My parents were very brave. They knew no one in America. What courage! I don't think I could do that."

"They were probably poor. One has to eat," she said.

He nodded. "They said we could be happy here. But I am dark-skinned"—he pointed to his olive skin—"so the Irish called me names. I didn't speak English very well"—his voice broke—"but I used my fists." He bent his fingers into a fighter's fist. "These are what pulled me through. Everyone listens to these." Excitedly, he kissed one fist, then another. "They are my jewels."

She watched him warily, afraid to look at him directly for his eyes were piercing. His lips curled in a flirtatious smile as he raised his strong chin and gazed at her. His high cheekbones flushed with a rosy glow. Above them, his eyes drew her in again. She felt as if his eyes undressed her in public, as though he knew everything about her. Her heart pounding, she tore her eyes away from his.

"I must go," she said, hastily gathering her packages.

Courteously, he helped her to her feet. When he touched her arm she felt a tingling sensation but tried to remain calm.

"May I carry those for you?" he asked.

"No," she blurted out. "I'm sorry. I appreciate it, but . . ."

"Your husband won't like it?" he said quietly.

She nodded, conscious that the Italian women nearby were watching every move.

Regally, he took her hand and kissed it.

"Francesca, you are very beautiful," he said softly.

Glowing under his admiring gaze, she bowed her head modestly.

"A Madonna!" he sighed.

When he released her hand she trembled.

"I must go," she said.

She walked quickly down the path, in a hurry to get home. The way the Italian grapevine worked, she knew that her husband could find out about this chance meeting very soon.

Because he was a cop in the West Village, George Giotti hated the fact that he was Italian. The Irish dominated the local station house and barely tolerated him. Fortunately, George liked to drink, which amused his buddies. They whispered that he was a dago and everyone knew that dagos knew members of the Mafia, the illegal society against which the police vowed vengeance.

The Irish cops didn't get upset at crooked politicians, nor did they particularly care about other groups selling drugs and running houses of prostitution. Only Italian crimes of murder and violence excited them. These evil blots on mankind must be eliminated.

But the police did not dent the power of the dark arm of Italy. It was a black cloud over the city, controlling all phases of the entertainment business, restaurants, hotels, gambling, prostitution, and drugs.

The drug business was causing a rift in the *padrino* network. Don Guido Allegro did not want his family to deal in this area. But the Young Turks like Tony Tucci approved of this lucrative vice.

The police knew that Tucci was moving to control drug distribution on the East Coast. They also knew that Don Allegro had no sons and thought of Tucci as his heir.

Would Tucci's move cause a rift in the Allegro family? The police hoped so, because if there was a full-scale war, they might have a chance to infiltrate the Mafia and break their strength.

The key was getting information, which was difficult because no one talked—not even honest Italians. The community could witness a murder, then zip up their mouths when the cops arrived.

This frustrated George's efforts. He passed on the gossip about the rumblings in the Allegro family to his superiors. But Captain Lafferty wasn't impressed.

George wanted a promotion badly, so he drank at

the Hudson Street Tavern instead of going home to Francesca. Over whiskey, the cops talked about whores and showgirls—the perks of being a cop. All hookers put out for cops. His buddies talked about sex as if it was distasteful. They never talked about sex with their wives. Wives and mothers were sacred.

George did not fool around. As far as he knew, all hookers carried diseases. Besides, he could have his wife whenever he wanted. Now that she was pregnant, she resisted. But he insisted. After all, a real man controlled his woman.

Tonight he was loaded. He bade a drunken goodbye to his buddies, mentioning that his beautiful wife was waiting for him. Weaving and bobbing, he walked down Hudson Street, calling out to neighbors. When he reached home he slowly climbed the stairs to his apartment. When he passed his sister's apartment, the door opened.

"Jesus, Tillie, get that stuff off your eyes," he demanded.

"I'm married, and my husband likes makeup," she said defiantly.

"Get it off, Tillie."

Patiently, she took a handkerchief from her apron pocket. She spit on it, then rubbed her eyes, causing them to blacken with mascara. Looking like a wounded doll, she grabbed George's arm.

"I have something to tell you."

"What's that?"

"I heard from Carmen, the woman who works in the five and dime?" She waited until George nodded. "It seems that Francesca was in the park talking to Tony Tucci."

George's body froze.

"What the fuck are you saying?"

"Carmen called a few minutes ago. She said the whole neighborhood is babbling about Tony Tucci. He's paying court to your wife!"

"Francesca?"

"She's nothing special. Tucci has women all over the place. He's fooling around with that truck driver's wife. Aldo won't say anything because he's scared shitless."

"Stop cursing," George shouted. "Women don't use that kind of language."

Warily, she stepped away from him. His mood turned ugly as he stomped down the hall.

"Carmen said that Francesca was smiling and being friendly to Tucci," Tillie called after him, smacking her lips with great satisfaction. She did not like her uppity sister-in-law.

"I'll take care of this."

Intuitively, he touched his gun. Tillie ran after him.

"George. You're not going to do anything foolish, are you?"

"Mind your own business."

"Sweetheart, leave the gun with me. You know how bad your temper is. Leave the gun here, in case you forget yourself. Please?"

George stared blankly at his sister's pleading face. Her request made sense. He whipped out his gun and gave it to her.

"Keep it safe," he said.

When he unlocked the apartment door he heard music on the phonograph. He took the record and smashed it on the table.

Startled by the noise, Francesca appeared from the bedroom dressed in a bra and panties.

"Come here, you bitch," he said.

She grabbed for a housecoat, managed to get it on, and ran for the door. His face was swollen with drink, and there was rage in his eyes. He grabbed her, his hands holding her fast. She struggled like a pretty bird in flight as he smacked her hard.

"I told you to behave. I don't want you talking to any man. Do you understand?"

His hand was so heavy that when he smacked her again she fell to the floor.

"Talking to a mobster? What the hell do you think you're doing? I don't want you to go out of this house, do you hear me? You stay home after I leave in the morning and you be here when I come home at night."

"I have to see my mother," she protested, her lips bleeding from his blows.

"Damn!"

He kicked her, careful not to touch her womb for the sake of his child. She screamed with pain.

There was banging on the door.

"George, get control of yourself! Don't hurt the baby!" Tillie screamed.

George picked up Francesca and carried her into the bedroom. He shoved her onto the center of the bed and smacked her until her beautiful face was a mess of blood. Then he tore her bra and panties off. He dropped his pants, rammed his penis into her, and fucked her good. That would teach her to behave. After he finished George rolled over and snored.

Beside him, Francesca lay with her hands on her womb, comforting her baby. Her mind was racing.

Somehow she had to get away or one day she would kill her husband. And no one would understand what drove her to commit an insane act like murder.

No, she must escape before she lost control.

In his sleep, George threw a heavy hand on his wife's body. Francesca struggled under his possessive gesture. He would never let her get away from him. But she had to, for her baby's sake.

She thought about her baby. Certain it was a girl, she chose a wonderful name: Victoria Regina. The name conveyed power, something she wanted to give to her daughter.

Francesca wept for the future life of her baby girl.

She must save little Victoria Regina. But how?

Then she thought of Tony Tucci and the gentle way he had spoken to her. He was a powerful man—a man afraid of no one. Could he help her?

Exhausted, she fell asleep and dreamed of different ways of killing her husband. When she awoke, her entire body was filled with violence.

❧ *Chapter 9* ❧

*T*ony Tucci thought of seventeen-year-old Francesca constantly after the day he introduced himself in Washington Square Park. He walked through the park daily, hoping for another glimpse of the young mother-to-be.

Tony felt cursed because he preferred living on the edge. The danger of his business gripped him and was the reason he chose the life of a mafioso.

But in his personal life, ecstasy eluded him. He had affairs with many women. Showgirls. Models. Actresses. But women eventually disappointed him. They needed praise, reassurance, and love, so he lavished them with expensive gifts.

His current mistress, Maria Cortina, was no exception. As long as he gave her diamonds and cash, and paid her bills, she was happy. Maria rolled her eyes, licked her lips, pouted for kisses, and was easy to please.

Tony suspected that Francesca was different. How wasteful to shower her enormous beauty on George Giotti, who could never appreciate her. It's no wonder Giotti was jealous and kept Francesca at home.

Tony felt frustrated. An affair with a married Italian-American woman required diplomacy because of his stature in the community. The Mafia flourished because of its rigid rules. This illegal group did not interfere with honest Italian-American citizens. Although most members of the community were God-fearing, they tolerated the Mafia because the Mafia made sure there was no rape, mugging, or robbery.

To keep this balance, Tony's personal behavior must be respectful. His current mistress was susceptible to his seduction, and her husband did not complain, so Tony was not condemned. Instead, the blame focused on Maria.

Very ambitious, Tony was known to be tough as nails and had been dubbed Tough Tony. Without hesitation he enforced decisions eliminating enemies of the Don. His day-to-day battles were carried out by henchmen, but Tony reported directly to Don Allegro.

Childless, the Don regarded Tony as a son and urged him to live at the compound in Bayside, Queens, where tall gates surrounded five stone houses. The Don's three married sisters lived in neighboring houses. People whispered there was a curse on the family because like the Don, none of his sisters had children.

The Don had one single sister and hoped Tony

would marry her. But Tony felt that marriage was personal, not business.

Besides, from the day he saw Francesca Giotti's beautiful Florentine face, Tony had a plan.

The only way for it to work was to wait until Francesca had her baby. It would be a sin to rob her peace of mind while she nurtured a new soul. In six months the birth would take place, and Tony could make his move.

Giotti was no problem; the Mafia knew how to deal with cops. They were all the same—interested in cash. Giotti's bulging pockets would convince him to step away from his marriage. And he could have his child as a bonus. Tony did not want to share Francesca with another man's child in his home.

He spoke to no one about his plan and spent his days feeling crazed, as if he had been struck by lightning. After looking into Francesca's beautiful face he was smitten, and he sensed that she felt the same way.

Tony patiently redecorated his Fifth Avenue apartment and bought clothes, jewels, and furs for the woman he wanted.

She would be his when the time was right.

He waited with great anticipation for the right time to arrive.

"Get away from me. Leave me alone," Francesca said.

"I'm sorry, honey. I really am. I don't know what gets into me. I don't mean to hurt you. I love you, you know."

Wearily, Francesca looked into George's dark eyes.

When he put his hand on her shoulder she shuddered to get away from him.

"You can't drink, George. You turn into an animal."

His gaze turned arrogant as he rose from the couch. He went into the kitchen, opened the fridge, then slammed the door shut. When he returned to the living room he walked back and forth.

"You're not like other wives," he said spitefully.

"How are other wives?" she asked.

"They forgive their husband. You don't. You never forget anything."

She pointed to a bruise on her arm.

"How can I forget?" she asked.

Sheepishly, he put his hand on his forehead, shaking his head. It was not his fault. If she was a good wife, he would never lose his temper.

He sat next to her and caressed her cheek. But she moved away from him, frightened. He put his arm around her shoulders, and she began to cry.

"Don't," he pleaded, caressing her.

She raised her head, sobbing. Tenderly, he wiped away the tears on her cheeks.

"I'm sorry, honey. Oh, God, I'm sorry. What can I do to make it right?"

Her sobs softened, but she looked at him warily.

"Do you mean that?" she asked.

"Of course I do. I love you."

"Then stop drinking.'

He looked wounded. He shook his head violently.

"I can't do that."

Her shoulders slumped in defeat. Determined, she tried again.

"Then think of the baby. The doctor says I need

fresh air every day. You won't let me out of the house. It's not good for our baby."

He hung his head, ashamed.

"You're right, honey. I'm sorry. I'll try to do better."

"Then I can go out during the day? Take walks? See my mother?"

His heart froze. She was so eager. Was there another man?

"George?"

"Yes, honey?"

"Is it okay?"

"Sure."

He laid his head against her breasts.

"Forgive me. Please, honey."

She was silent. After a while she went to bed. When he tried to caress her, she moved away.

Two men were following her. Francesca walked into the sausage shop and watched them take a position in a doorway across the street.

"What can I do for you?" Mr. Perillo, the butcher, asked.

"A pound of hot sausage."

He looked at her with concern.

"It's not good for the baby," he said.

"My husband likes hot sausage," she said.

"Okay. But let me put two pieces of sweet sausage for you."

She smiled at the plump man who was the father of seven children. When the package was ready she paid for it quickly. She left the shop and headed toward the park. As she walked she looked into shop windows and checked the men. They were still there.

By the time she reached the park she was frightened and ducked into the ladies room. It was empty except for Jamie, who was repairing her lipstick in the sink mirror.

"Hi there, Francesca. Haven't seen you in a while."

"I've been staying home," Francesca replied.

"Pregnant?"

"It's obvious, isn't it?"

"You're not that large. I'll bet you're happy," Jamie said warmly.

Francesca looked into the mirror. She was pale. She suffered from constant nausea and pain. She ate to calm her stomach and gained too much weight. Her slim body was bloated, and she was always uncomfortable. When she walked she felt off balance.

But she wouldn't give in to her discomfort. Every day she cleaned the apartment and cooked dinner. The doctor said that long walks in the sunlight would help.

"Let's sit and talk," Jamie said, taking Francesca's arm.

They walked across the park and chose a secluded bench. Francesca looked at the green lawn. She would love to sit on the grass and roll over on the cool ground. Instead, with great effort, she lowered herself gently onto the bench.

"I'm a little clumsy," she said to Jamie.

"You're fine. When do you expect the baby?"

"About two months."

"Bet you can't wait till then."

"You're right," Francesca said.

Again she spotted the men. They wore fedora hats

with tilted brims to hide their faces. She began to shake.

"Are you okay?" Jamie asked.

"Those men. They've been following me."

Jamie looked at them.

"Are you sure?"

"I saw them at Bleecker and Tenth Street. I stopped in shops, and everytime I came out they were waiting."

"Do you have any idea who they are?"

"No."

"I'll talk to them."

Francesca grabbed Jamie's arm.

"They might hurt you."

"Don't worry, Francesca. I can take care of myself."

Jamie sauntered over to the men and spoke to them. Startled, they moved away from her, but she grabbed one of the men's arms. His hand went into his coat pocket. Watching, Francesca wondered whether he had a gun. Jamie kept on talking. Finally, she returned.

"Don't worry. They're friends of a friend," she said.

"What does that mean?"

"I don't really know. That's what they told me." She paused, looking at Francesca curiously. "They said you'd know."

"I don't know what they mean," Francesca replied. Her head was pounding. She turned toward the American girl. "I want to thank you for doing that. I wouldn't have had the nerve."

"That's what friends are for," Jamie said, smiling.

Suddenly Francesca's reserve melted.

"I'd like to be your friend," she said shyly.

"Me, too," Jamie said.

To distract her, Jamie asked Francesca about the baby. Francesca said that she thought it could be a girl. The teenagers talked about movies and found they liked many of the same ones. It didn't take long for Francesca to relax and feel more like a young girl than a pregnant woman.

"This is fun," Jamie said.

"Girl talk," Francesca said.

"What's wrong with that?"

"Nothing."

"I come here every day, Francesca. Why don't we meet and gab? It'll be good for you. You're walking around carrying that baby. You need some fun."

"I sure do," Francesca said.

"It's not easy to be a mother," Jamie said.

"Oh, no. I think being a mother is the most wonderful thing in the world," Francesca said eagerly. Then she checked her watch. "Oh, I've got to go home now."

"Righto! See you tomorrow."

As Francesca wound her way home she checked to see if the men were still following her. They were. Again she stopped at several shops, but the men followed her until she reached home.

When she entered her apartment she put her packages down and slipped off her shoes. Then she undressed and sat on the couch.

Francesca had not answered Jamie's question, but she knew who her friend was. She breathed deeply and felt safe now that Tony Tucci was protecting her.

*   *   *

Maria Cortina sang as she worked. She was on the roof of 242 Thompson Street. Her husband, a truck driver, liked his shirts dried in the sun. She liked to keep Aldo happy, for he was a good man, though he was a failure in bed.

When Maria found love with Tony Tucci, Aldo pretended that it wasn't true. His friends whispered that Maria was unfaithful, but he shook his head and said that Maria was a good wife.

Maria was very careful not to embarrass Aldo and visited Tony at the Hotel Fifth Avenue, in the suite of rooms he kept. Occasionally, when Aldo was away, she went with Tony to uptown nightclubs. On those nights she changed into an evening gown at the hotel and wore the diamonds Tony gave her.

Maria liked the double life she led. In the daytime she was an ordinary housewife, washing her husband's shirts, cooking his meals, buying groceries at the local stores, gossiping with women. By night, when her husband wasn't home, she led the life of a glamorous mistress to a powerful mafioso. It was exciting. Plus she was stashing money and jewels in a safe deposit box for her future.

Maria was very practical. She knew that Tony could not be hers forever. When he left her she planned to settle comfortably into middle age with Aldo.

Lately she had spotted signs of Tony's restlessness. At the beginning of their affair he wanted her all the time. Now their affair was routine, and their passion had lost its glow.

Though she expected his love to fizzle, Maria was jealous. Last night she told Tony she was sure he was in love with someone else. That's when she realized just how dangerous Tony's anger could be.

She vowed to be careful, for Tony was not an ordinary man. He was a mafioso.

She hung the shirts on the thick line. She was so intent upon her work that she did not notice the movements behind her. Suddenly the line was pulled down and wound around Maria's neck.

Maria's body was wracked with spasm. The rope was drawn tighter and tighter until all color left her face. Blood erupted from her mouth, her nose, and her eyes. Then, with one shuddering jolt, all life left her body.

Maria's corpse fell into the pile of carefully washed shirts, and her blood spotted the clean white fabric. Her mouth was open, her eyes were staring at the sky. Her face embraced a look of perpetual fury at the sudden twist of fate that had transpired.

Chapter 10

She is lovely,'' Jamie said to Francesca.

"My Victoria Regina," Francesca murmured at the little bundle in her arms.

"Visiting time is over," Sister Anne said.

St. Vincent's Hospital was very strict about visits between mothers and babies. The nun, dressed in the white and blue uniform of a nurse, smiled at Francesca.

"She'll be back soon," she said, scooping the baby up in her arms. As she did, Francesca blew a kiss to her baby.

"They'll probably call her Vicki when she goes to school," Jamie observed.

"I hope not. I'm going to insist on Victoria Regina."

"That's a long name for kids to swallow."

Francesca's eyes lit up. It had been a hard birth,

twenty-four hours of labor. When the baby finally arrived she was exhausted.

"Is George happy that you had a girl?" Jamie asked.

"George says he doesn't care. He hasn't been back to see Victoria Regina. He's probably drunk. His sisters check in every day around noon. That's why I told you to come at five. They're always hanging around, spying."

"Still? What's there to spy about?"

Francesca gestured to two large bouquets of flowers on the bureau.

"Gorgeous. Who sent them?" Jamie asked.

"There's no card. Tillie and Anna suspect you know who. I pleaded with them to throw the flowers away before George visits, but they refused. They said it was their duty to tell their brother everything about his wife. What kind of women are they?" She shook her head in silent rage. "I was going to ask Sister Anne to throw out the flowers. But then I felt it's not *my* fault if a certain person wants to send me flowers. I haven't done anything wrong."

"Francesca, have you spoken to George about Tony Tucci?" Jamie asked.

"George spoke to me. When that poor woman died, George brought home the *Daily News* and shoved it in my face. He said, 'Is this the kind of man you like, a man who has people killed?' " She paused. "Listen to who's putting Tony Tucci down. George is fast with his fists, but that's okay because I'm his wife. Anyhow, the *News* said that it wasn't a mob rubout. But that poor woman, dying like that, on the roof, alone. It was awful."

"All the more reason you must be careful. You don't want to get involved with Tony Tucci."

"My mother says the Mafia never hurts women. She says the killers could have been Aldo Cortina's friends."

"So you're still thinking of Tucci?"

Francesca blushed. "He's different from George. He's really interested in me. George is only interested in himself. He's either reprimanding me or begging forgiveness. All he wants is supper on the table, a clean house, and my legs open every night," Francesca said bitterly. "Jamie, if I go on like this, I'll be dead before I'm thirty. Or I'll kill him. There's no way out. And I have Victoria Regina to think of. I have to save her from George's drinking."

"Get a divorce."

"How can I? I'm Catholic!"

"George is Catholic, too. Yet he beats you up whenever he feels like it. And he rapes you."

"Rapes me? No." Francesca's face flushed with denial.

"That's what having sex against your will is."

"But he's my husband."

"Oh, Francesca, I feel so much older than you."

"Jamie, I like you, but you have strange ideas sometimes."

"No, Francesca. Your ideas are strange. For some reason you think you have to obey this man. You're in America now, not Italy. My cousin is a good lawyer. He'll help you out of your marriage."

Francesca bent her head. "I can't do that. It would be a sin."

"But you just said that you won't be able to live with George without doing something awful."

Francesca's body heaved with sadness.

"Maybe there's another way," she said.

Jamie examined Francesca, who wore a look of sadness, but also one of hopefulness. Affectionately, Jamie kissed her cheek.

"I'd better go. Your mother will be here soon, and she doesn't like me."

"Thanks for the gift," Francesca said. "The baby will love the rattle."

"Tell Victoria Regina that Aunt Jamie will give her lots of gifts. Now that I'm writing a book I can afford to spoil her."

"What's the book about?"

"Us," Jamie said. "Nighty night."

In the Village Café the smoke was misty, dimming the effect of exhilaration on the faces of the people who flocked there. Every night was a party for those in search of sensual ecstasy invented in the twenties, documented in the thirties, politicized in the forties, and changing the entire scope of sophistication in the fifties.

Jamie was cavoting in the center of the crowd, equipped with a diaphragm, a checkbook, and an attitude that made anything possible. Tonight she was celebrating. A publisher had given her a contract for her new book, *Bourbon in the Boudoir*. It was a racy book that followed its heroine to many European watering holes and was a decidedly feminist tract. The heroine went to bed with every son of a bitch who delighted her, all in the name of sexual freedom. The editor had told Jamie to tone down the sex, but she refused. They still bought the book, knowing the sexual climate of the country was changing and that her novel would create a sensation.

Jamie kissed Fernando, the Spanish painter she had slept with the previous night.

"Let's go home," he said, wanting to bed down because he rose early to paint his large abstract-expressionist canvases.

"Not tonight," Jamie replied, watching a dark-eyed Greek poet.

"Are you going to break my balls?" Fernando demanded.

"Fernando, dear, I didn't say we were on for tonight, did I?"

"Ballbreaker," he muttered, and he moved toward his steady, an artist's model who greeted him with open arms.

Jamie moved toward the gorgeous poet surrounded by three women, uptown models who were downtown for a bit of fun. Jamie swaggered her leather-clad hips, lit a long cigarillo, and muttered a deep hello. Fascinated, the models watched Jamie's seduction of the Greek.

"You're a writer, aren't you?" the Greek said. His name was Alexander, and everyone called him Alexi.

"Yes, I am," Jamie said, her deep eyes hidden by dark glasses.

"I've heard you're good in bed," he said.

"That's what I've heard about you."

Suddenly he put his arm around Jamie. Her leather jacket creased under the strength of his muscular grip.

"Do you live nearby?" he asked.

"Right up the street," Jamie said.

"Let's go."

The regulars at the bar smiled as Jamie walked out of the bar with her new conquest. Women envied her. Men envied him. Oblivious to the furor they caused, the couple swung their arms around each other and, laughing, left the smoke-filled place. They walked up MacDougal, where Italian bars and bohemian cafés clustered on the narrow street. When they reached Jamie's apartment house they ran inside quickly. Five flights up, in Jamie's large apartment, Alexi whistled.

"This is a great place for a party," he said, looking around.

"I'm glad you like it," she said.

He surveyed the walls filled with abstract-expressionist paintings, then walked into the next room, where rare books filled the shelves. In another room a typewriter, a desk, and a large poster of Michelangelo's *David* competed with a poster of Matisse's *Reclining Nudes*. Down a long hall was a large bedroom. The bed was covered with a silk print spread. There were brocaded pillows and a plush red velvet canopy reminiscent of Matisse's Algerian period.

"I love it all," he shouted.

He pulled off his black sweatshirt with the head of Ezra Pound printed on it. Underneath, his muscular chest swelled with desire.

Jamie tossed her leather jacket on the floor and quickly removed her boots and jeans. Underneath her T-shirt she wore a lacy bikini set. It was black and provocative.

"What's your book about?" he said, as he placed her in the center of the bed.

"It's about a beautiful Italian woman I know," she replied.

"You mean you're not in it?"

"I didn't say that," she laughed. "I'm in all the racy parts."

"And she?"

"She's a symbol of repressed womanhood," Jamie explained.

"Poor girl," Alexi said.

"Don't worry. I intend to save her," Jamie said seriously.

Then they laughed as they swept each other onto the path toward ecstasy.

Chapter 11

*F*rancesca sang to her sweet baby, who was lying in a crib next to the kitchen table. The morning sun was bright, and the baby smiled as she played with a bracelet from Jamie, a gift for her first birthday. Time had passed very quickly.

Victoria Regina was gurgling "mama," which thrilled Francesca. In the bedroom, George was sleeping late because it was Saturday. Francesca enjoyed this private time with her daughter. Seated in her pretty blue and white chair, Victoria Regina had swallowed two mouthfuls of peas when the doorbell rang.

Thinking it was Matilda, Francesca rang back. When she went out into the hall she saw a delivery man on the first landing.

"Yes?" she called out to him.

"Giotti?"

"Yes."

"Packages for you."

She watched him climb the stairs carrying two large packages.

"I haven't ordered anything," she said to him.

"Your name is Giotti, right?"

"Yes."

"Sign here," he said, handing her a receipt.

"Could you carry them into the kitchen?" she asked after signing for the packages.

The delivery man carried the two large boxes into the kitchen and looked at Victoria Regina. "Cute," he said. He tipped his hat and left.

"What's all the noise about?" George was standing at the bedroom door, scratching his head. "What are they?"

"I don't know."

He checked the slips on the boxes. "Giotti. That's us."

"They're probably gifts for the baby's birthday."

"Who sent them?" he asked, his eyes examining the boxes.

He took a knife from the cupboard and slit the packages open. In the first box, wrapped in lots of pink tissue paper, was a teddy bear much too large for a baby. George opened the second box. Inside was a lovely crib, imported from Italy, with lovely angels painted on it.

"This is expensive stuff," he said. "This can't be from your family."

"I don't know who sent it," Francesca murmured.

"What do you mean, you don't know?" he demanded, brandishing the knife.

Her body tensed at the rage in his voice. In the last

year she had learned to avoid George's rages. Sometimes she was successful, sometimes not. Always, she did what she had to because of her baby. What would happen to Victoria Regina if she died? She had to leave George and take Victoria Regina with her.

"Don't touch me," she shouted.

The windows were open because it was a warm day, but Francesca knew that, though neighbors might hear her screams, no one would interfere between a husband and wife.

"You're my fucking wife," he said, smacking her hard.

"Stop that," she screamed.

He curled his fist and hit her on the jaw. She fell, weeping.

"Never talk back to me," he shouted.

"I'm going to call the police," she threatened.

"*I'm* the police." He laughed. "You've been talking to your friend again. I'm going to fix that whore. She's putting too many ideas into your head."

"Think of the baby," she pleaded.

He put a hand under the baby's chin, but Victoria Regina began to cry.

"My little Vicki," he said. "Sweet innocent baby. Not like her whore mother."

He turned to Francesca and beat her savagely. She put her hands over her face, but he tore them away. In a few minutes her nose was bloody, her eyes puffy, her lips split and swollen. She lay on the ground sobbing. Satisfied, George went into the bathroom.

With every ounce of her strength Francesca pushed her body up. She stumbled toward the baby but was shaking so badly she was afraid to hold her. She crawled out of the apartment and down the stairs. When she reached the street she hailed a taxi.

"You okay, lady?" The driver peered out of the window. "Want to go to a hospital?"

"Take me to 130 MacDougal," she said.

In the rear of the taxi Francesca tried to stop the bleeding. When she reached Jamie's apartment house she realized she had no cash.

"Please wait," she begged.

In the entrance hall she leaned on Jamie's bell until Jamie buzzed back. She opened the door and called out to Jamie. When Jamie reached Francesca she was shocked.

"That bastard!" she swore. "We're going to the hospital."

Jamie helped Francesca back into the taxi and told the driver to go to the St. Vincent's emergency entrance. Once there, Jamie helped Francesca into the emergency room. Immediately, an intern came to their aid.

"What happened?"

"Her husband beat her," Jamie said.

"Wait here," he said, taking Francesca with him.

Two hours later a nun came out of the emergency ward and spoke to Jamie.

"We're going to hospitalize your friend," she said.

"I want to report this to the police," Jamie said.

"Will she sign a complaint?"

"Yes."

"We'll have to notify her family. Do you have their telephone number?"

"Please don't. They'll call her husband. He's a cop, and—"

"A cop?" The nun's eyes opened wide. "You'll have trouble. You know how the police are."

"Damn."

"Are you a relative?" the nun asked.

"No. But there's a child, and—"

"Has he hurt the child?"

"Not yet."

"Dear," the nun said sweetly, "I know you mean well, and I sympathize. Do you know how hard it will be to get the police to interfere, if her husband is one of them?"

"Isn't there some way?"

"She can go to Family Court. It's the only way." The nun smiled sympathetically. "Why don't you go home now? Come back in the morning," she said.

Jamie was falling asleep when she heard a loud banging at her door.

"Police. Open up," a coarse voice called.

She put on a Japanese robe and walked to the door.

"What's wrong?" she asked.

"Open up," the voice demanded.

When Jamie opened the door the violent face of George Giotti stared at her. He was accompanied by another policeman.

"Is she here?" George shoved Jamie aside.

"No."

"I don't believe you."

He stalked through the apartment. Satisfied that Francesca was not there, he returned to Jamie.

"Where is she?" he demanded.

"I don't know," she said.

George hit her across the chest with his nightstick.

"Listen, you creep," Jamie screamed, "touch me again and I'll have my lawyer—"

"What's that you have?" George said to his buddy.

Nick Panto grinned. In his hand he held a white envelope filled with heroin.

"Possession of heroin. Let's take her in."

Jamie stared at George.

"You son of a bitch," she cursed.

He hit her again with the stick until she fell to the ground, unconscious.

"This will take care of the little bitch," George said as he and his buddy carried the scantily clothed girl down the stairs and put her into the police car.

❧ *Chapter 12* ❧

Francesca sat up in her hospital bed listening to her mother speaking in whispers.

"George will take you back if you promise never to disobey him again. Francesca, you must think of your baby."

"Victoria Regina." Francesca's lips hurt as she said the name of her baby. "Is she all right?" Her eyes were filled with fear. "Has he touched her?"

"George is not an animal," Matilda said. "He's a man who lost his temper, but he could never hurt his child, I swear to you. Your father and I talked it over, and it is the only thing to do. Go home and beg forgiveness. George will show mercy."

"I can't do that."

Matilda's face contorted with a mixture of fear and anger. She seemed to be at war deep inside herself. Finally, she spoke in a compassionate tone of voice.

"My daughter, you ask for trouble. A woman's duty is to be a good wife and mother."

"And a man's duty? Is it to beat his wife each night? Is it to take pleasure from her body as if she is a woman of the street?"

Matilda's arms folded in an impeccable mixture of resignation and anger.

"I told your father that George drinks too much. But he says, 'My daughter made her bed, and she has to lie in it now.' "

"I didn't make my bed. You made it for me. I didn't want to marry George."

"I thought that was simply the fear of an innocent sixteen-year-old. I thought . . ." The woman's head bent, and her eyes were teary. "Was I wrong to urge you to marry? Your father was obsessed with your purity. I thought, once Francesca is married, he will relax." She shrugged her shoulders in defeat. "He wants nothing to do with your domestic problems. He is probably right. It is your marriage. We should stay out of it."

"I'm not going back to George," Francesca said slowly.

The effect of her words hit Matilda hard. Her body recoiled as if she had been physically hurt.

"How will you accomplish this?" Her mother's face was contorted with rage at life's unfairness. "You have no money. I have a small amount, but it won't help you for long. Of course, I'll give you all I have."

She beat on her breasts in a solemn oath. The sweat from her fists moistened her black cotton blouse. Her dirndl skirt was black, too. She was wearing black because she was mourning her daughter's suffering.

Francesca always presented Matilda with insoluble problems. On the one hand, Matilda was proud of Francesca's spirit. To crush this would turn her young daughter into a washed-out woman. But, she also knew that this spirit could cause her much pain, given the customs of their world.

"The important thing is that I have to get Victoria Regina and leave here. Do we have family anywhere? Someone who can help while I get an annulment?"

"But you can't get an annulment. You have a child."

"I'm going to ask a priest about that. I think when a man forces himself upon his wife, there is something that can be done."

Matilda shook her head violently. "No. No. There is nothing to be done."

"Don't say that," Francesca said hysterically.

Her head rolled back and forth as if she were having an epileptic fit. Matilda put her hand on Francesca's forehead to calm her. Francesca's eyes were wild with anguish. Her hands fluttered like captured birds hoping for escape.

"There is no hope," Matilda said grimly. "Women have no freedom except in death."

"So I should die? Well, I won't. I'm going to live, and I'm going to find a way."

"There is none," Matilda said.

"What happens in Italy when a man brutalizes his wife?"

"In Italy a woman has brothers who reason with the husband."

"And if he does not see reason?"

"There are times when a woman returns to her

family with her children. But she lives like a widow. She never goes out, except with her family. She has no friends. All she does is raise her children.''

"And her husband?" Francesca asked.

"He lives a normal life. He can travel. See women. See his children.''

"And legally?"

"There is no divorce in Italy."

"There is in America."

"Not for people like us. Francesca, you must stop thinking that you are different. You aren't.''

"I am different. I see things differently. I hate Papa. He could stand up to George.''

"Your father is a disappointed man. If you had a brother, you might have a chance. But your father refuses to interfere. He feels that George is a policeman. He has the law on his side.''

"So he's right to beat me?"

Her mother sucked in her breath before she said the next words.

"Your father says you probably deserve it. He knows how rebellious you can be. He says he wanted you to marry because he saw the signs of trouble. You and your fancy ideas. All that glamour, those magazines, the movies. He says I spoiled you, letting you dream." Her voice fell. "I wanted you to have your dreams while you could.''

Matilda bent her head, and tears streamed down her cheeks. Francesca wiped them away with her fingers, but her mother shook her hand away.

"No, don't be kind to me. I knew when you became a woman your life would be hard. What woman doesn't know that?''

"My friend Jamie says that we don't have to live this way. She says—"

"Your friend is rich. Besides, she is a *putan*. The whole neighborhood talks about the men in her apartment."

"She's modern."

"She's a whore and a drug addict."

"Drugs? Never!"

"She was arrested for having heroin in her apartment."'

"That's not true. Jamie drinks a little but she never takes drugs."

"How do you know? Besides, George made the arrest."

"George?"

Francesca began to shake.

"What's the matter? Nurse! Nurse! Something is wrong with my daughter," Matilda shouted.

A nurse appeared at the doorway. She went to Francesca's bedside and checked her pulse.

"She shouldn't be upset," the nurse said pointedly to Matilda.

"I feel better," Francesca murmured.

"All right. But visiting hours are almost over."

The nurse left them alone.

"He did it to punish her," Francesca muttered.

"What do you mean?" Matilda whispered.

"Don't you see? Jamie said she'd help me if I leave George. So George arrested her on a false charge. My husband is a real bastard, Mama."

"You see how men always win. It does no good to fight them." Suddenly Matilda checked the time. "I must go. Your father will be home, and he likes his food ready."

"I'll be all right." Francesca tried to cheer up for her mother's sake.

But her mother was not fooled. Her wide brown eyes were troubled as she smoothed down her blouse, checking for the cross around her neck and placing it outside the blouse so that everyone could see it. Then she bent and kissed her daughter goodbye.

"Things will change. You'll see. They won't seem terrible when you feel better. George will behave. Remember, think of your baby."

After her mother left, Francesca thought of the sweet baby to whom she had given life. Now Victoria Regina was an infant. In ten years she would be a girl. In twenty she would be a young woman. What would her life be like if Francesca did not separate her from George's brutality? No, she had to escape George. If not for herself, then for Victoria Regina's sake.

But her mother was right. The world was controlled by men. And there were no men in her family to defend her against George. There was only one way to escape. She must have the protection of a man of great power, the kind of power that could combat the efforts of the New York City Police Department. For if she tried to escape George, he might resort to the kind of thing that he had done to poor Jamie.

Jamie would survive. Her rich family could take care of her. But Francesca? If her husband had her arrested, who could come to her aid?

Since she was a little girl Francesca had heard the screams of wives punished by their husbands. Women screamed in the middle of the night and the next day wore long skirts and long-sleeved blouses to cover the embarrassing bruises. Other women consoled them, but no one ever called the police. What would happen if the police were called? The women whispered that the police respect the law of the husband. Wives have no rights.

Women tried to get help for their friends. They talked to the priest and to relatives. The brutal husband was admonished, and for a while things were quiet. Most times the brutality continued when men drank too much.

Why didn't the law help women?

Francesca lay there, her eyes closed, searching for an answer. She must escape George. If his sisters liked her, she could ask them to talk to George. But they hated her and adored their brother. There was no one to appeal to about George's behavior.

She needed the help of a powerful man. Someone who could stand up to both George and the police department.

She knew who that man was.

She bent her head and silently thanked God that there was someone who could help her. She had only to ask him.

🐵 *Chapter 13* 🐵

*I*t was Sunday morning. Tony Tucci picked his way through the crowd leaving St. Anthony's Church on Sullivan Street. A constant flow of people milled about. Many lined up outside the cheese store to get the fresh ricotta and other delicacies made in the basement.

Next to the cheese store was the convent where the Franciscan nuns lived. The curtains were covered with Irish lace because the nuns were Boston Irish who volunteered for missionary work among these Greenwich Village Italians. Like their missionary forebearers in colonial Africa, the nuns had nothing in common with the people they came to save.

Next to the convent was Zampiere's Bakery, where fresh onion pizza was a Sunday favorite. A moan escaped the crowd when the baker announced he was sold out. Everyone complained. Why couldn't he bake more onion pizza? Each Sunday he ran out. But the baker was stubborn.

After breakfast the ritual Sunday visits began. Every family had a sister, brother, or cousin living in the wilds of New Jersey, Brooklyn, or Queens. Families took the long treks on subways to wherever their relatives lived. When they arrived back in the Village, they were relieved. The Village was close to everything important: Macy's and St. Patrick's Cathedral.

As Tony rubbed elbows with churchgoers women smiled and men bowed formally. Older women kissed his hand as he tucked ten dollar bills into their purses. Everyone knew that Tony Tucci was a generous man.

"The man has real class," one woman said to another.

"He is a man among men," a man whispered to his wife.

"He really cares about us," an old woman murmured.

Tony did care. His crisp new bills were always handy. His manner was friendly. Because of his position in the Allegro family, he walked with bodyguards. But not here, among friends. On Sullivan Street Tony felt no harm could come to him.

He walked slowly toward the tenement where his mother lived. She preferred to live here, though she occasionally visited him in his large Lower Fifth Avenue apartment, which overlooked Washington Square Park and the South Village Italian enclave.

Quickly, he climbed the stairs to the first floor apartment where his mother waited. She was dressed in a somber black dress, and the gold of her cross, wedding band, and earrings shone against her pink skin. On a beautiful embroidered tablecloth were a bottle of wine, a bowl of shiny fruit, and freshly baked cakes decorated with sugar—Tony's favorites.

"Mama," he whispered, holding her close.

"My son."

"How are you?" he asked.

They sat at the table as she recited a litany of family gossip. One daughter is pregnant. Another has money problems. A son cheats on his wife. Another son has problems with his oldest son. The litany went on. Afterward, Tony settled some problems with money. Some with advice. For the problems that couldn't be handled easily, he told his mother what to do.

This was his role in the family, for he was the eldest son.

"Is that all?" he finally asked.

"There is one thing more, my son." She hesitated. She never discussed his business, knowing that it might upset Tony. Besides, who was she to judge? Her priest said she should love her son and pray for his soul. And who knew better than a priest about saving souls?

But this time she must speak. She had waited a long time, but it was time for her words to be heard.

"It's about Maria," she said.

"What about her?" he asked grimly.

"There is talk that you had something to do with her death."

"Why would I hurt Maria? She was very good to me."

"They say that you tired of her."

"Perhaps, but I did not have to kill her, did I?"

"They also say that one of your business associates harmed her."

"We do not harm women," he said.

"Then who?"

He shook his head. "Some say it was her husband or his family."

"Such a brutal way to die."

"There is no good way to die, Mama, except a death of honor." He paused. "There is nothing I can do about Maria. The police will find her murderer."

"Are you sure?"

"I despise men who brutalize women. It is the act of an animal."

"I know that," she said, her wrinkled hand grasping his elbow. "Now, my son, what do you have to tell me?"

He was not surprised. His mother could always read him very well.

"I'm going to be married," he said.

She clasped her hands with joy.

"Who is it?"

"Francesca Giotti."

Her body contorted as she defended herself against the trouble that life often handed her. Then her body became a shield of armor. She was tough and experienced with life's brutalities. She knew how to deal with them. Her face wore a look of stoicism and courage.

"My son," she said finally, "she is a married woman and a mother."

"Her husband brutalizes her. She cannot stay with him."

"He is her husband."

"She was only sixteen when her father forced her into this marriage. She can get an annulment based on that fact."

"But she has a child."

"The Church has annulments for these kinds of marriages, though it may take some time."

Antoinette Tucci knew that her son's mind was set.

"I am happy for you, my son," she said.

"The gossip in the neighborhood—will it make you unhappy?" he asked gently.

"I do not listen to gossip. Besides, they would not dare insult you to my face."

"I'm sorry, Mama."

"Tony, must you marry this girl? Isn't there someone else? Someone who is free of complications?"

"I love Francesca," he said calmly.

His mother knew that he had never said those words before.

"I love you," Tony said to Francesca.

Her pale face brightened and two pink spots appeared on her cheeks. She looked fragile lying in the hospital bed. The doctors were concerned because her strength had not returned. Because of her severe weakness they were taking more tests.

Her bruises were real. She told the doctors that her husband beat her. Did she want to call the police, they asked. She said her husband was the police. They nodded, understanding, and kept her in the hospital.

"I want to marry you," Tony said.

Francesca looked into Tony's deep blue eyes and lost herself in a world that seemed pure with love. Her heart beat fast. Slowly, Tony's lips touched hers, conscious of the swelling of her mouth. He kissed her gently, though his body hardened with desire.

Her hands tenderly touched his cheeks, softening the look on his face. With her gesture, part of his armor crumbled. He gazed with rapture into the purity of Francesca's eyes, for she had captured his heart.

"I will take care of everything," Tony whispered, holding her close.

Francesca put her head on his shoulder and sighed happily. These were the words that she yearned to hear.

❧ *Chapter 14* ❧

*F*rancesca looked approvingly at the decor in the nine-room apartment she shared with her new husband—her first real home.

When she left the hospital Tony rented a suite of rooms in the Fifth Avenue Hotel at Tenth Street and Fifth Avenue. After petitioning the Church for an annulment, he learned that it might take years before action could be taken. So Tony persuaded Francesca to fly to Reno for a six-week divorce.

At first Francesca refused.

"I am Catholic," she said. "I cannot get a divorce."

The lawyers explained that it was only a temporary measure. Tony was exerting pressure, and the Church would grant an annulment soon. Besides, while she was George's legal wife he could sue for divorce at any time and name Tony as correspondent. The lawyers explained that Tony must be beyond the arm of the law because of his business activities.

Francesca thought long and hard about marrying Tony. There was no doubt in her mind that she loved him. Was she sinning by wanting this man? Tony said no, that they had a right to be happy. Wasn't God merciful?

When she spoke to Tony about his "business" he explained that most of his ventures were legal, so Francesca stopped asking questions.

Tony's mother, Antoinette, showered Francesca with affection and wished them happiness.

Her own parents, on the other hand, were difficult. Bruno refused to see her, but Matilda secretly visited whenever she could.

The lawyers told Francesca that there was no possibility that she could gain custody of Victoria Regina. They tried to barter with George for visiting rights, but he refused. They pleaded that Victoria Regina should know her mother, but George replied that Francesca had abandoned her child to live with a known mobster, and he did not want his daughter's life ruined. George had all the weapons he needed. His sisters could testify that Francesca was a neglectful mother, and everyone in the Village knew about her dalliance with Tucci while she was married.

Every night Francesca wept for her daughter. Yet oddly she felt happy, too, for she was experiencing being truly loved for the first time.

Tony gave her anything she wanted. Clothes. Jewels. Furniture. He brought her gifts to remind her of his love.

Respectfully, he waited until they were legally man and wife before he made love to her.

Their first weeks of love were dreamlike. When Francesca responded to Tony's touch she was filled with a new joy. When his lips touched her nipples, instead of contracting in fear, as she often had with George, Francesca felt a moistness surge through her as she pulled Tony closer to her, kissing him wildly.

Francesca began to like sex as they spent weeks exploring each other. Night after night, in the mornings and afternoons, their wild excitement built to excruciating pleasure, and she screamed "Tony, Tony" in his arms.

When Jamie remarked on Francesca's glowing appearance, Francesca confessed that she had never dreamed she could be so happy.

Jamie fought the trumped-up heroin charges with the help of her prominent family. Since she had no previous record, she was given a probationary sentence. Francesca and Jamie often saw each other, though Tony warned his wife: "Remember, Jamie is not Italian. She does not understand our customs."

Francesca had invited Jamie for lunch. Francesca loved to cook in her modern kitchen. The white vinyl tiles on the floor and the asphalt tiles surrounding the stove were tidy. The kitchen was different from her mother's, although there were the Italian touches— the garlic and peppers hanging from the ceiling—which contrasted with the modern red crockery and stainless steel pots and utensils. And in the sleek new refrigerator there were slabs of prosciutto, salami, and provolone.

While she worked the phone rang.

"It's a gorgeous day. Let's forget lunch," Jamie said. "Meet me in the park."

"All right," Francesca agreed.

Francesca walked quickly through the kitchen, passing her hand over the color-coded cabinets, the push-button oven, the sleek plastic laminated countertops.

She walked down the long foyer to the living room. This room looked as if it was part of a modern ranch. The slate floor, the cork tiles, the walnut ceiling beams, the fireplace of massive stones, and the simple couch and chairs gave the room an open spaciousness. It was not like living in the city.

She walked into the modern bedroom where fiberglass curtains divided the sleeping space and two dressing areas. Inside her dressing area she chose a tan linen suit with high notched lapels, narrow waist, square shoulders, and swing skirt. She slipped into it, then clipped on pearl earrings, slipped into brown and white spectator pumps, and donned a white straw hat.

She examined her reflection with wonder. Only a year ago she had no choices. Now she could pick and choose furniture, clothes, anything she wished. Her life had changed completely.

But she had lost something very dear.

Each afternoon Francesca strolled in Washington Square Park, hoping to see her daughter, Victoria Regina. The child was almost two, and Francesca swore someday she would have her daughter back. She pleaded with Tony, but he replied there was nothing he could do.

When Tony was not there, Francesca wept for her baby. She was guilt-ridden. But she consoled herself by thinking that George loved the child and would take care of her.

Through her mother, Francesca kept a constant check on Victoria Regina. George hired a neighborhood woman, Lila, to care for her. The child was always spotless. Lila watched over her carefully. Still, Francesca was not allowed to speak to Victoria Regina.

She tried to. Lila said, "I'm sorry, Mr. Giotti says you cannot speak to the child." So Francesca sat on a nearby bench and watched Victoria Regina play. Kindly, Lila did not tell her employer, for she understood Francesca's sadness.

"Here I am!" Jamie waved to Francesca when she entered the park.

"Is she here?"

Jamie pointed to a nearby playground where Victoria Regina played in the sandpit. Lila was close by.

Francesca nodded to Lila, who smiled.

"She's darling," Francesca said, watching Victoria Regina fill a pail with sand and then turn it over. Lila fussed over the child, cleaning the sand from her body.

Victoria Regina was not a pretty child, but there was an appealing delicacy to her. Her milky complexion heightened the impact of her red hair and hazel eyes. But her expression was not a child's, for she wore a look of sadness.

When she saw Victoria Regina Francesca wanted to take her into her arms and kiss away that sadness, to tell her baby that she loved her and that they would be together.

The denial of this impulse caused Francesca's body to cave in. Her shoulders slumped, her head bent, her expression was forlorn, and her heart felt heavy with hopelessness.

Sitting next to her, Jamie put her arm around her friend.

"Don't worry. Someday you'll be able to tell Victoria Regina that you love her and that her bastard father was the one who kept you from her."

"But I did it myself."

"What do you mean?"

"If I was a good mother, I would have stayed with George."

Jamie gasped.

"Don't you remember what he was doing to you? You wouldn't have lasted long. Francesca, you did the right thing."

"I lost my baby."

"Just for a time. You'll get her back. The lawyers will think of a way."

Suddenly Francesca's body jerked.

"What's that on her leg?"

Startled, Jamie looked carefully at Victoria Regina's legs. "Oh, my God," she said. "He's hitting her. That bastard."

"I must go over." Francesca rose to her feet.

"Don't," Jamie restrained her. "The last time you went over to her, Lila did not come back to the park for months. Do you want that to happen again?"

Francesca sat down hesitantly.

"I'll go over," Jamie said.

In her black leather jacket, boots, and dark glasses Jamie created a stir among the mothers in the playground. Quietly, Jamie spoke to Lila. The woman nodded. Then Jamie went over to Victoria Regina.

"Hello, there," she said to the two-year-old, "you don't know me, but I'm your adopted aunt."

As she spoke to Victoria Regina Jamie noted that the child had not inherited her parents' good looks. Damn fate, Jamie swore. She knew Victoria Regina's life would be difficult, and a pretty face could be an advantage.

She kissed the child on the forehead. Then she returned to Francesca.

"Well?"

"She has a bruise. George told Lila that she had a fall. I think that's baloney." Jamie pressed her hands together, cracking her knuckles. Then she curled her hands into fists. "George will get away with it again," she said sadly.

"Tony will do something, I know he will."

Francesca pressed her fingernails into her hands, tearing at her skin.

"He won't," Jamie said sternly. "He can't afford to."

"But how can he do nothing?" she asked, her eyes filled with tears.

Tony held Francesca's hand tightly. He placed her hand to his lips and kissed one finger at a time. They were cuddling on the living room sofa. The terrace doors were open as they watched the sun set over the city.

Each day Tony came home for dinner promptly at six. Afterward they sat together for a while. Then he made love to her. When she slept, he left for his nightly activities around the city, not returning until the early hours of the morning.

"I have something to tell you," Francesca whispered. "Something that will make you very happy."

"You make me very happy," he said.

"You're going to be a father."

The elation he felt was sudden, a surge of emotion shooting through him, causing tremendous excitement. He grabbed her roughly, too excited to be careful.

"My darling, are you sure?"

"Yes. The doctor confirmed it today."

"I am blessed," he moaned.

He went down on his knees before her, put his head on her lap, and wept. Finally he could speak again. "This will make things right for you," he said, wiping the happy tears from his face.

"What do you mean?"

"This will heal your sadness about Victoria Regina."

"No, Tony. It will not. I will never be happy until I have my daughter."

Tony felt enormous sadness. He loved Francesca very much, but the one thing she yearned for he had to deny. He did not want another man's child in his home. Especially not George Giotti's child.

"It is impossible, my darling. The law is on Giotti's side."

"I think he's beginning to hurt Victoria Regina," she said. "If I'm right, won't the law take her away from him?"

"Who will tell them? You know how people feel about interfering."

"I will report him."

"But you can't prove anything, Francesca. Giotti

will say that you were a bad mother and wife. He will tell the court that you're married to me. What court of law will take your word against a cop's?"

"Then the law stinks," she said bitterly.

He held her, rocking her body gently as she cried.

"Don't worry, Francesca," he promised. "You will forget."

"A mother can never forget her children, Tony. Don't you know that? That would be a sin against nature. I will always love Victoria Regina."

PART III

NEW YORK CITY

---Early Summer---
1988

VICKI

❧ *Chapter 15* ❧

*H*ow we doing?'' Vito said to Vicki in her office. ''Have a chocolate chip?''

He held out a bag of cookies, but she grimaced.

''For breakfast?'' she complained.

He laughed and tossed an envelope on her desk.

''Have you seen the latest shots of the crazy mafioso?'' he joked.

Vicki opened the envelope. The photographs were of a middle-aged mobster wearing a robe and slippers while strolling on a Greenwich Village street.

''That's Carmine Solari,'' Vito said. ''He owns a beachfront house in New Jersey. A waterfront Miami estate. An East Sixty-fifth Street townhouse, between Madison and Park avenues. And he walks around MacDougal Street in a robe and slippers every night.''

''Why?''

''He's watched by the feds and wants them to think

he's nuts. He's not. He runs most of the Mafia business in Brooklyn but wants the entire East Coast."

"That's Tucci's territory."

"Right. Tucci and Solari grew up together and went to the same schools. They both worked for Don Allegro, but Tucci inherited the Allegro family after the don died. Solari was given the Brooklyn action, but he's become dissatisfied. He wants more, so he's trying to annoy Tucci."

"How?"

"Tucci has this thing about how a mafioso must always be a gentleman. Dress well. Be polite. That kind of thing. Solari's acting like a fool in public is embarrassing to him."

Vito paused for a moment. He loved to talk about the Mafia. He hated them, but the drama of the organization and the dynamics of their membership fascinated him.

"Tucci and Solari may be in a real head-to-head battle for leadership. They have very different styles. Tucci thinks of his role in the Mafia as his destiny; he feels a responsibility to be a generous, classy guy, which Solari doesn't feel. Solari belongs to the new group of guys who want to change the Mafia ballgame. The old mafiosi were absolutely loyal to authority. Remember the rule of *omerta*? It meant silence until death. The old mobsters really believed that. And they lived up to the idea of glamour. The big hats. The sharp silk suits. Cuban cigars. Italian shoes. Showgirls for mistresses. They wouldn't be caught dead looking like this guy." He pointed to Solari in the photographs.

"I guess the Mafia is experiencing the same deterioration of values as the rest of the country," Vicki observed. "Don't the Feds call them Yupsters now?"

"They do," Vito answered. "Yupsters are the younger wiseguys who are mainly interested in their bank accounts. They're fighting the Colombians, the Jamaicans, and other gangs for the drug market. Because the Feds have put so many of the older wiseguys away, the Yupsters are moving up the ladder too quickly. And they're making wrong moves."

"What do you mean?" Vicki asked.

"Remember that hit on West Broadway the other day? The shooter was on a motorcycle when he sprayed the stretch limo with bullets. That was much too public for the old Mafia."

Vicki pondered Vito's information as he paced her office. His face was flushed, and his dark brown eyes glowed with exhilaration. She touched him affectionately. "Calm down," she said. "You're going to burn out."

"Look, when I went to school everyone thought I was related to a mobster because I had an Italian name. I hate those guys."

"I know."

"They're animals. In the past five years there have been fifty hits. Tucci is surrounded by young wiseguys who want to become capos. They're willing to kill anyone. They're watching the black gangs getting rich overnight, and they want in on that action. Tucci doesn't like the drug business, but he's not going to be able to control this new element. That's the weakness we're going to use to get him."

"Why does Tucci murder so many of the old guys?"

"He's hard to figure out. What other mafioso allows

his daughter to become a sexy rock star? That's completely out of character. Mobsters are very strict with their families."

"Arianna is a good match for her father. She's a hard woman," Vicki observed. "A bitch on wheels. Tough as they come."

"You have problems with her?"

"When Mary Adams wrote that piece about Arianna's relationship with her father, she interviewed me. Arianna was furious. She said I leaked information from this office."

"Did you?"

Vicki looked sullen.

"I did mention some things off the record. But they were mostly gossip, not facts."

"Never trust a reporter, Vicki."

"I learned that the hard way."

The phone rang. Vicki picked it up, listened, then handed it to Vito.

"It's for you," she said.

He listened to the voice at the other end. Then his face broke into a smile. "Great!" he said. When he hung up, he clapped his hands.

"What happened?" Vicki asked, laughing at him.

"Good news. One of Solari's guys is ready to talk about the Vitale murder. Vitale is the guy who was hit in the stretch limo. Our snitch says the story is that Solari personally ordered that hit."

"Will he testify before the grand jury?"

"Yes. I want you to work on this with me. Okay?"

"Sure."

"Apparently Solari wanted to get rid of Vitale because he was nosing in on Tucci's Atlantic City business. Solari must have figured Tucci would owe him one. The snitch says that Tucci is well connected outside of the city. He says that Tucci even has friends in Hollywood. He's close with show business people.''

"Did he buy his daughter's career?"

"There was a lot of scuttlebutt about that. Basically, she did it on her own. People behind the scenes say that he pulled a few strings, but she's built a real following. Her Carnegie Hall concert is sold out." Vito pondered his next words. "She's talented. And sexy.''

Vicki's eyes narrowed. "Okay, why don't we set up a meeting with this snitch?'' she said.

Vito watched Vicki's demeanor change. On the job she was efficient and cooperative, but she kept her personal life a mystery. No one in the office was able to crack Vicki's professional facade.

But everyone whispered that they were sure that thirty-seven-year-old Vicki was still a virgin.

Inside Tiffany's Paul Johnson waited, watching the well-dressed women who were at home in the famous store. Because he often served as escort and lover, Paul had an eye for a woman's economic profile. Two women walked into the store wearing expensive T-shirts from Bill Blass. This fashion statement announced that they were women who had everything. Another woman wore a skirt with Lesage embroidery. This was an elaborate French needlework favored by the most expensive designers.

She smoothed down her skirt as she browsed. Displayed in a case were diamond frogs, carved jade butterflies, and ruby-and-sapphire fish. The woman seemed intrigued by a diamond-and-enamel serpent bracelet. Examining the piece, she sucked in her breath.

"Aren't they wonderful?" she asked Paul, noting his lean body.

Paul knew the look that conveyed that the woman needed an eligible bachelor. In Manhattan, the bachelor shortage was rampart. "Every man I know is either gay, married, or psychotic," one of his clients complained. Paul jokingly told her that there was actually a remote island in the Caribbean where thousands of eligible males were hiding. She hugged him and said, "You really like women."

He did, but, like the classic kid in the candy store, he liked different flavors and couldn't imagine settling on one. He was always very successful with women. One day it occurred to him that he had a marketable product. Instead of spreading it around—especially since the fear of AIDS was changing sexual customs— he decided to conserve his sex appeal. He'd use his sexuality for clients, charging an exorbitant fee to support his acting career.

That's when he discreetly communicated that he was available for a woman's needs. Since then he'd been very busy, but his acting career suffered because he hated to disappoint a client. Unfortunately, auditions were often called on short notice, too late to reschedule a woman in a romantic frame of mind.

He worked hard to create the illusion of romance for his clients and choose the right touch for each woman. He had convinced his newest client, Vicki Giotti, to meet him at Tiffany's so that he might create a romantic illusion for her. As an assistant district attorney, Vicki had a tough reputation. But her toughness was getting in the way of the one thing she wanted most: a baby.

He planned the fantasy: He was her ardent lover who wished to give her a lovely, expensive gift as a token of his love. Vicki laughed and said it was silly. When he reminded her that she was still apprehensive sexually despite his earnest lovemaking, she agreed.

Her reasons were pragmatic: She wanted a baby and knew that frequent sex improved her chances.

Paul's technique was aimed to make a woman feel human. Men could pay prostitutes and perform impersonally, but this did not work for women. Paul always planned a scenario. He had a great deal of experience. He serviced lustful women whose needs could not be met by their husbands, women who were frigid, and sometimes combinations of the two. For Vicki he created a two-target plan: enjoyment of sex and impregnation.

"Which one do you like?" the woman asked Paul, breaking into his thoughts. She pointed to the serpent bracelet, looked at Paul, and licked her lips with her pink tongue. Her body leaned against the counter, conveying sexual interest.

"They would all look wonderful on you," he said in a throaty voice.

Her cheeks turned crimson as he put his hand on hers. "Unfortunately, I'm waiting for someone. Do you have a card?" he asked with style.

Quickly, she produced a card from her snakeskin purse. He put it in his breast pocket as their eyes locked.

At that moment Vicki entered the store. He sized

her up expertly. She was slim and small-breasted. Her legs were curvy and quite sexy; Vicki wore short skirts and elaborate shoes to show them off. Her head was oval and regal; she walked as if she were a royal personage.

Her wonderful red hair was worn in an upsweep. Her lovely hazel eyes lit up when she spotted Paul.

"I'm late, aren't I?" she said.

He knew she was nervous and put his arms around her.

"Go with the fantasy," he whispered.

"You're the expert."

"Let's browse."

He led her to a counter where a diamond-and-pearl necklace was displayed. Next to it was a diamond watch and several diamond rings.

They moved to a counter that displayed hearts of every size. He'd already chosen a tiny gold heart for her.

"I'll take that," he said to the salesperson, and he held Vicki tightly as the woman put the heart in a blue Tiffany box. When it was tied with a white ribbon, Paul gave it to Vicki.

"Will this be on my bill?"

"Remember the fantasy," he whispered.

They left the store. Outside, he flagged a cab. Paul gave the driver Vicki's address and kissed her. She pulled away, embarrassed, but he kissed her again, pinning her firmly against the seat. When she resisted, he whispered, "Don't you want a baby, Vicki?"

"Here we are," the driver said ten minutes later.

Quickly, they entered the apartment house and took the elevator. Once inside her apartment they climbed the stairs to the second level of the duplex. "Take your clothes off and join me," he said gently. He disrobed quickly. He drew the blinds so that the bedroom was dark, then lay back on the plush bedspread.

"I'm waiting for you," he whispered.

She undressed shyly. Naked, she was beautiful, for clothes hid the soft curves of her body.

"Come here."

She sat at the edge of the bed as he reached for the combs in her hair. Her red tresses fell around her face, heightening the glow on her cheeks.

He put the heart around her neck and whispered, "I want you, darling."

As he held her, she softened. She kissed him like a little girl, with tightly closed lips.

From a bag he took a mask he had purchased earlier. "Here, put this on."

Nervously, she followed his instructions. The mask was blue with gold sequins. For himself he chose a black mask that conveyed mystery.

"Stand with me," he instructed.

They stood in front of a mirror as his hands explored her body until he felt her soften. Then the hardness of his body moved against her to stimulate her.

"I want you to put your lips on me," he said.

At first she moved away, but he held on to her firmly.

"Don't look at me, look into the mirror. Can you do that?"

She looked at the masked woman, and the image made her forget who she was. Paul's nakedness began to excite her. His body glistened with the sweat of sexual heat. In the center of his body his penis glowed. Paul took Vicki's hand and put it on his penis. She rubbed it, watching the penis turn from pink to hot red.

"Your lips . . ."

She bent over him, her long tresses tantalizing his body. But her lips were dry. He raised her head, put his tongue in her mouth, and circled it. Her legs moistened as she felt desire surge through her crotch.

"Do you want me?" he asked.

"Yes," Vicki moaned.

He flicked her vaginal area with his penis. Greedily, she grabbed it.

"First your lips. Be gentle," he coaxed.

Her lips opened for him, but she didn't know what to do, so he guided her with his hand on her head. Earlier she had confided that she hated men because her father had abused her. To earn her trust Paul knew he had to be gentle.

"That feels wonderful," he said.

But her lips barely touched his penis. Excited, Paul yearned to shove his penis into her. He removed her mask. Her face was pink from desire. He took his mask off. Their eyes locked, and he saw fear in her eyes.

"Darling Vicki," he crooned, "I'm not going to hurt you."

But she was shaking. Gently he turned to her and said, "Why don't you play with me?"

She rubbed his penis against her vagina, letting him enter her slightly. Whenever he tried to penetrate, she retreated.

He waited patiently, knowing she could not acknowledge that he was a real man with compassionate feelings.

She was an odd woman, a brilliant attorney, taking on tough cases. But in bed she was a frightened child.

Feelings for Vicki overwhelmed him. He must be careful. He could not allow himself to become emotionally involved with a client.

"Go ahead," he whispered. "Enjoy yourself."

Like a child with a toy, Vicki played with his penis. He penetrated her slightly, aching for pleasure. She resisted, and her fists pounded against his chest. Finally he inserted his penis into her, and the exciting friction began. Her legs went limp when he was inside. He pushed hard into her, whispering that she was beautiful. He grabbed her breasts, touched her taut nipples with his fingers, then his lips touched every part of her body, softening her.

When she cried out, tears covered her lovely face. Slowly, Paul kissed each one, whispering that he adored her.

❦ *Chapter 16* ❦

Six weeks later Vicki walked down Washington Street carrying a bag of groceries. Tonight she was going to prepare an intimate dinner for Paul. For several weeks she had talked to the Mafia informant, checking out his story. Though she had tons of work to do, she needed a night off.

Washington Street was very quiet. When Vicki was growing up, the street was unsafe. It was located too close to the waterfront, where muggers, transvestites, and other night dwellers confronted one another. The real estate boom changed things. Industrial buildings became luxurious cooperatives. But the tree-lined street was sparsely trafficked, except during rush hours when desperate motorists sought escape routes from the city.

Vicki turned into Jane Street and walked toward her apartment house. Suddenly a black Cadillac pulled up.

Two men jumped out of it and grabbed her. One put his hand over her mouth so she couldn't scream. Another quickly placed a blindfold over her eyes. Then they carried her into the car and wedged her between them. The car took off, heading down Washington Street.

She could not see anything and concentrated on the sounds in the room. Her hands and legs were tied tightly, so she could not sit comfortably. Fear consumed Vicki as she heard the steps of men coming toward her. In total shock, she urinated and was horrified at her body's loss of control. A hot flush surged through her because her kidnappers had witnessed this embarrassment. Mentally, she began a conversation to calm herself. Don't be hard on yourself, she thought, remembering how often she had used those words with crime victims. Fear created situations where loss of body control was common. She had witnessed many such incidents when both suspects and victims were questioned. Except when the perpetrator was a hardened criminal, the shock of crime wrought havoc on the people involved.

I must handle this, Vicki thought. She was familiar with severe discipline, for that was the premise on which she based her life. Sometimes Vicki felt her life was all about denial. Denial that she had sexual needs. Denial that she experienced uncontrollable anger. Denial that she had fantasies of killing her father.

If she admitted these feelings, she was not a "good" person. She wasn't sure whether it was Catholicism or her strict upbringing that taught that she could never be "bad."

She forced herself always to be a lady at great cost to her emotions. She deadened her feelings to be an effective prosecutor, to make her reputation in court as an attorney to be reckoned with. She liked her reputation as a hard-nosed bitch who knew her law, could charm her juries, showed respect to the judges, and won her cases.

She never lost a case.

Her reputation filled other lawyers with awe. There was no one in the office who had her batting average. She flaunted it like an ornamental crown.

"Okay, kiddo," a voice said. "We want the name of that creep who's talking to your people. Give it to us and we won't say a word about where we got it. Okay?"

Now she knew who she was dealing with. The Mafia. She was surprised. Generally, they left prosecutors alone. It was witnesses they killed, making it difficult for attorneys to get people to talk.

"Make it easy on yourself," another gruff voice said.

"We're going to get it one way or the other," the first voice added.

She said nothing.

"Okay."

The first blow shook her off balance, and her body fell to the ground. Immediately she went into a fetal position. Blood erupted from her nose. She felt its heat as it covered her lips, her chin, then her neck. As the blood flowed she felt helpless.

Her urine-soaked panties reminded her that under all the professionalism, the discipline, the bitchiness, she was still a frightened little girl.

The men laughed. One kicked her, and pain seared through her body.

She screamed again, then bit her lips and tried to hold on. Another harsh blow landed on her face. A kick in the stomach filled her with nausea. She prayed that she was not pregnant.

"Are you all right? How do you feel?"

Vicki blinked. Her body felt as if it was broken in two. She was only partly conscious.

The sheets felt itchy. They must be synthetic. Because she suffered from an allergy, she slept on expensive cotton sheets. Cotton sheets that made her feel like an Egyptian queen in a crypt, journeying to the next world.

The place smelled of antiseptic, bodies, and fear. I must be in a hospital, Vicki thought. Her panic rose. Had she been badly hurt? She couldn't take it if she was seriously injured. She didn't want to need help from anyone.

She screamed, "I will *never* need anyone."

"Take it easy," someone said.

Vicki focused. A nurse stood beside her bed.

"Where am I?" Vicki asked.

"St. Vincent's Hospital. The police are waiting to talk to you. How do you feel?"

"Anything broken?" Vicki asked.

"You have a broken rib," the nurse said. "Don't worry. It'll heal quickly."

The nurse left, and two policemen entered. One began talking. He blinked nervously as he wrote in a notebook.

"I'm Officer Carstairs. My partner and I found you near the waterfront. What happened?"

"I'm Vicki Giotti, an assistant district attorney," she explained. Her lips were swollen, so it was hard to speak. "A couple of wiseguys picked me up. They tried to beat information out of me. It's about a case I'm working on."

"What can you tell us?"

"They picked me up near my apartment. I was blindfolded, so I don't know where they took me. They asked me questions and beat me up," she said matter-of-factly.

"They must be pros. They could have killed you," Carstairs noted.

"They wanted to scare me, not kill me. But I didn't tell them a thing," she boasted.

The nurse appeared again. "You must sleep," she said to Vicki. "The doctor gave you a shot."

Then the blackness took over.

It was a blackness that was familiar to Vicki. She retreated into it whenever she was afraid. In the blackness there was a beautiful mother who protected Vicki. They lived in a fairy-tale land with a castle, a moat, and a blue sky. She was a princess, and her mother loved her very much.

Whenever her father hurt her, young Vicki ran into the bedroom and locked the door. He banged on the door, shouting for her to come out. But she wouldn't. When everything was quiet, Vicki had to decide whether her father was waiting for her or whether he had fallen asleep. Half of the time she guessed right. Panic swept through her small body as she left her safe haven. If her father was on the floor in a dead heap, she could breathe easy.

Sometimes he was waiting and pounced on her. That's when the blackness and the castle and the beautiful mother did not work. That's when she reached out for the mother who was not there.

Television reporter Mary Adams put the last touches on her lead story: *Mafia breaks its rules. Assistant District Attorney Vicki Giotti assaulted because of her involvement in a Mafia investigation.*

Mary wrote the story easily. She had received a tip from a nurse at St. Vincent's emergency ward when Vicki Giotti was brought in. Apparently she was in bad shape. Mary bet she'd be back at her job in a few weeks. Vicki Giotti was a strong woman who relentlessly pursued her convictions.

When Mary confirmed the story with Vito Marchese, he told Mary that the district attorney did not want Vicki's face on television. For this reason, he asked the press to bury the story. Would Mary cooperate?

"Sorry," she said.

But she wasn't sorry. It was her lead story on the six o'clock news.

❧ *Chapter 17* ❧

*L*et's kick ass," coach Kelley screamed at the players in blue and white uniforms.

They were cops who were donating their time to raise money for the Police Athletic League. The audience consisted of mothers accompanying children. The women looked annoyed at the coach's display of macho strutting and jock language.

"Way to go," one player screamed at the man at bat. When the hitter swung at a pitch the ball careened high, then dropped into the pitcher's glove.

"Get him out of there," Don Morton yelled.

He was standing on the sidelines next to his buddy, George Giotti. George patted Don on the back.

"It's only a game," he said. "Take it easy."

"You never used to be this calm," Don remarked, guzzling a beer.

George watched the beer foam cover Don's lips. In

the past hour Don had consumed half a dozen cans of beer. George's lips felt very dry. His stomach was lurching, and his head felt heavy. Sweating, he jumped up from the bench and walked a few feet. His hands were shaking and his legs trembled, sure signs of panic. Time to go to AA, he thought.

"Gotta leave," he called out to Don.

His friend looked puzzled. "Hey, Georgie, the game isn't over."

"Things I have to do," George muttered.

Don laughed, knowing that retired cops usually looked for things to do to fill their days.

It was true. Since his retirement two years before, George felt useless and depressed, a fact he kept secret from the AA group. Though he was counseled to share his moods, feelings, and thoughts, George never spoke at AA meetings, because all the years as a cop trained him never to reveal anything.

He attended the meetings. Noon meetings. Meetings at three P.M. Meetings after dinner. Afterward, he walked the streets until he was weary. Then he went home to watch television all night. Without booze, George couldn't sleep. All night long he worried about what he'd do the next day. Except for brief visits with his sisters, George spent most of his time alone. When he tried to make a date with Vicki, she complained that she was too busy.

It was his own fault. A cop's life was hard on marriage. Many marriages ended in divorce because of the impossible hours connected to the job. Some of George's buddies married again or lived with women. Some moved to Florida, collected pensions, and worked part-time as security guards. Some went fish-ing. All complained that they missed the action of the New York streets.

George walked those same streets, but out of uniform it wasn't the same. When he saw rowdy crowds, when he saw pushers, he closed his eyes. He was sick and tired of that filth. But aside from walking the Village streets, George had nowhere to go.

Because he'd be tempted to drink, George couldn't visit his old haunts. AA policy said that whenever he felt panic he should go to an AA meeting.

Nowadays he thought about Francesca constantly, remembering how beautiful she was and how tasteful she looked. Not like his sisters, who teased their hair and painted their faces like whores.

He still loved his wife. Damn her! Why did she leave him? Something was wrong with her. That's why she caused his anger. It was her fault for letting him lose control. He wouldn't have touched a hair on her head if she hadn't provoked him.

When she ran into Tucci's arms, George planned to kill them both. But he resisted the impulse, knowing that Vicki could not survive the tragedy.

He was proud of his daughter because she dedicated her life to law and order as he had. Though he had trouble showing it, he adored her.

The streets were peaceful west of Seventh Avenue. On the corner of Charles Street George looked into the large windows of a popular Spanish restaurant. Because it was daytime, the restaurant was half-empty. At night it was jammed because it was noted for excellent food and Spanish music. George stared into the window, noting the restaurant's quiet atmosphere. At the bar there was a large color television set. Suddenly, he saw Vicki's face flash on the screen. He rushed into the restaurant.

"Can you turn that up?" he asked the bartender.

The tall man shook his head.

"It might annoy the customers."

George handed him a ten-dollar bill, but the man shook his head.

"That's my daughter," George said, pointing to the bruised face on the screen.

Immediately the Spanish man turned up the volume.

"This is Mary Adams," the pretty reporter said. "Tonight at six we'll have the exclusive story of Assistant District Attorney Vicky Giotti's kidnapping and assault."

Oh no, George thought. Attentively, he listened to the reporter.

". . . and members of the Mafia may be involved in this assault."

Angrily, George banged his fist on the bar. How dare they touch his daughter?

The bartender walked over to George.

"A drink?" he asked.

George shook his head, though his body was trembling with desire for alcohol.

"Bastards," he whispered.

"Señor," the bartender said. "There are ladies present."

George laughed. He knew lots of ladies: housewives, shopgirls, waitresses, all willing to put out for a handsome cop. They weren't ladies, they were whores.

He walked out of the place. Instead of heading for the AA meeting he turned west, toward home. In the apartment he had a collection of guns. There was a special gun that was perfect to kill Tough Tony Tucci, who was behind this vicious attack on his darling Vicki.

Could Arianna Tucci do it again, or was she last year's glitzy pop princess? Was the popularity of her first album a fluke? It had sold five million copies worldwide and spun off her famous single, "Getting Ready for You." Did she have the sheer talent of a born performer, or did she simply have beginner's luck?

At thirty-six, was she finished? Her last album had sold only one million copies. Maybe she had spent too much time as the punk princess of the Lower East Side. She didn't sign with Aries Records until Jo Jo Johnston, her co-writer, said that she was ready.

Last week *Billboard* had mentioned the disappointment of her last album. The article, wondering about Arianna's future, worried her.

"We need more marketing magic," she said to Stu Sawyer. "Get on the ball. You're my agent."

They were sitting in Arianna's white living room. The bright sunlight gave a tropical look to the room, accentuating the bamboo plants and the soft pastel paintings, the only colors in the pure white atmosphere.

"Arianna, everything will be okay, I promise you. You've run into bad press. That television report by Mary Adams didn't do us a world of good."

"That bitch."

Arianna twisted her lovely lips into an unattractive smirk. It was late afternoon, and she wore a short black dress that rose above her knees as she sought a comfortable position on the plush white couch.

Next to her, Stu's gaze was hawklike. He began rhapsodizing.

"Don't worry, darling girl. We can overcome it. You have everything you need. Once in a long while someone like you comes along. It's not only your talent, it's your beauty. You're so goddamned balanced. You're strong, yet feminine. You're the woman every woman wants to be. You're the gal most men want to be seen with."

Stu admired Arianna's deepset wide eyes and her chiseled chin. As she moved her skirt hiked up to her exciting thighs. He studied them, then moaned.

"Don't sit like that, Arianna, please," he begged.

She laughed, deliberately spreading her legs and resting her elbows on them.

"If I was a guy, I'd sit like this." She glanced downward. "After all, I'm a very bad girl, aren't I?"

Her arm slithered up behind him, her long, brightly painted nails playing tap-tap along his shoulders like miniature wooden soldiers traveling to war. Again he moaned. Arianna was not only beautiful, she was obsessed. She was a woman who loved and sang about her experiences. Even among the jaded people in the music business Arianna's affairs and caprices shocked.

But she was strangely moral. She was adamant about never using drugs or alcohol while she worked. She didn't smoke, either, which made Stu happy. Too often, rock stars abused their bodies. As a result their careers were destroyed early.

Tight-lipped, Stu talked about strategy.

"We need positive publicity, darling," he said, grabbing her fingers. He put them up to his lips and nibbled on them one by one. Finally he put a few into his mouth and sucked them.

Laughing, she retrieved her hand from his mouth.

"Look, you knew what you were getting into when you took me on. I'm a star, but I've been controversial from the beginning because of my father."

Her voice quivered as she continued. "My father is unbelievable. He strangles me with his protection. Papa's guys are always shadowing me."

"Don't tell me that," Stu said nervously. He had been Arianna's agent for several years and didn't like to think about Tough Tony Tucci.

"My father isn't a murderer," Arianna suddenly defended. "He's a mobster, a street warrior, a mafioso, but he doesn't dirty his hands with murder. He has this image of himself as the protector of the innocent. Old women come to him with their problems. If they need money, he gives them cash. If their husbands are abusing them, he talks to the guys. If it's their son or daughter, he sends them messages about honoring their mother. The women adore him. They kiss his ring whenever he walks down the street. They feel protected with a mafioso in their midst. Whenever Papa visits Nanna, the neighbors line up to smile at him. They think if he smiles back, their lives will be blessed. They hold up their babies so he can touch them. If he kisses a baby, they think that baby's life will be miraculous."

Suddenly she gasped for breath. "How would you like living with that kind of father?" she asked.

Stu was nervous about Arianna's connection to the

Mafia. As a performer huckster, he came in contact with mobsters from time to time. He tried to avoid them whenever he could, but if they marched into a star's dressing room and told the star what to do, that was it. The Mafia could blackball any performer, anywhere. That's the kind of clout they had in the music business.

Several years ago he had met Arianna, heard her sing, and fallen madly in love with her talent. After she signed with him he received a visit from her father's henchmen.

"Do right for Arianna Tucci, or you're a dead man," they told Stu.

Well, he would do anything for her, because Arianna was a great star.

He waved his hand in midair for quiet. He must deal with present problems.

"Let's talk about the concert. We must choose your songs with extraordinary care," Stu said, wiping his forehead. "We have to show off your versatile talents. How about a soulful ballad? And then a mellow one."

"I'm writing a new song with Jo Jo," Arianna announced happily. "It's a real sizzler. And I've sketched out the costume I want to wear while singing it. Look."

She handed him a well-drawn sketch of a tight silk jersey dress adorned with mink bows, brightly colored buttons, and polka-dot bands around the waist and on the sleeves. With it, she sketched a polka-dot bandanna and matching gloves. Attached to the low-cut neckline was a bright pink safety pin. The entire ensemble would glitter because the dress was layered with a soft net adorned with sparkling sequins.

"That's outrageous!" Stu exclaimed.

Suddenly the doorbell rang.

"I'll go," Arianna said.

Stu followed Arianna down the narrow entry hall. The hall was stacked with boxes from Saks Fifth Avenue, Lord and Taylor, and Bergdorf's, results of Arianna's shopping for the concert. There were hatboxes, shoeboxes, and smaller boxes that contained accessories of every size and shape. There was a stack of glove boxes, because Arianna had decided to add gloves to her outfits for this concert. She said it was the ladylike thing to do.

When Arianna opened the door a television camera faced her.

"Yes?" she said sweetly, knowing that the television crew recorded every gesture.

"How do you feel about the fact that your father may be involved in the kidnapping and assault of Assistant District Attorney Vicky Giotti?" Mary Adams shouted in Arianna's face.

Arianna's movement was quick. Without changing the smile on her face she lifted her leg and pushed at the knee of the cameraman. He lost his balance, sending Mary Adams down the steep town house stairs. Arianna, still smiling, waved at the camera before she shut the door.

On the other side of the door she turned to Stu with a look of anger on her face.

"When is the press going to stop hounding me?" she shouted.

Stu put his arms around Arianna and held her trembling body.

"Never," he said softly.

Her head fell like a doll's that had been chopped from the rest of the body. Stu was right. She was Tough Tony Tucci's daughter, and no matter how big a megastar she became, people like Mary Adams would never let her forget it.

❧ Chapter 18 ❧

St. Anthony's Church on Sullivan Street opened its doors on June 10, 1888. The church was designed by architect Arthur Crooks, who used the Romanesque style popular in Italy. One hundred years later the Italian community was still proud of its beautiful church. With its tall green marble columns, its stained glass windows, and its lovely mosaics behind the main altar, the church was often used for film and television shoots. Its popularity was simple: Like everything Italian, St. Anthony's Church communicated drama.

The statues placed around the church were in a dazzling array of styles. When a worshiper entered this holy place there were many saints to choose from. This practice reflected the Italian peasant belief in magic, rooted in pagan customs and early Christian doctrine—a distinct contradiction to the American Catholic Church.

In most Italian homes there were red horns over doors, supplemented by pictures and statues of the Madonna and various saints liberally displayed throughout. In many rooms a shrine was set up with religious candles burning around a statue of a favorite saint. Often these shrines were adorned with dried palms from the most recent Palm Sunday mass.

These customs were repeated in St. Anthony's Church, where a conglomerate of statues, sculptural styles, altars, and candles were made available to everyone.

At the rear of the church was a particularly regal statue of the Madonna. This Madonna had very blue eyes, was very slim, and wore a bright blue robe and veil. The Italians complained that the statue was not in the popular Florentine style. As a result, people often did not worship there. Yet it had a devoted small following, especially among the older women who wanted a quiet place of worship.

Signora Luisa Di Giuseppi was one of them. At ninety, she was the oldest active member of the parish of St. Anthony. Signora Di Giuseppi filled her long days by volunteering her services for everything from answering the phone in the parish office to spending many hours at this altar, praying for her family and friends.

Today was warm, yet Signora Di Giuseppi wore a long black dress, as had been her custom for the last sixty years. On her head she wore the black lace veil her mother had given her when she was sixteen years old. Slowly, she walked to her favorite altar. She held black rosary beads in her right hand, and her fingers moved up and down the beads as she walked. Her eyesight was slightly impaired, and the church was dim, so the Signora was not clear, when questioned later, as to exactly what she saw.

She knelt on the bench before the Madonna. Her eyes closed as she concentrated on her daily prayer: to help her leave this life with as little pain as possible.

Something warm touched her knee and startled her. At first she thought it was an insect, though it was rare for one to be in the church because the custodian was fastidious.

Slowly she opened her eyes and looked down at her knee. When she saw the bloodstains, she thought impossibly that the blood was coming from her body. Am I dying? she wondered. She picked up her skirt to investigate, but she saw nothing. She stood up, straining her eyes to locate the path of the blood.

That's when she saw the body spread-eagled behind the Madonna. The man's chest and forehead were a bloody mess.

The Signora turned and fled to the door, running head-on into the priest who was entering the church. She could not speak; instead, she took him to the altar of the Madonna and showed him.

Policeman Joe Welch and his partner, Larry Rodriguez, headed for the steps of St. Anthony's Church where neighbors, spectators, and a television camera crew waited. Unfortunately, someone had tipped off the media that there had been a Mafia hit in St. Anthony's Church. It was a sensational story because it was the second time the illegal organization used this place of worship for one of its hits. The first time was twenty-six years earlier, when a policeman had killed a Mafia don and his henchmen.

"Has the body been identified?" Mary Adams assaulted the policemen with a microphone. Next to her the television camera recorded.

"No comment," Welch said politely.

He and Rodriguez walked up the steps to the entrance where Father Reilly waited. The priest had locked the church doors. It was the only reason Adams wasn't inside, filming everything.

"That lady is a vulture," Father Reilly said when the policemen reached him. "I had to lock her out. Imagine!"

"Thanks for doing that, Father," Welch said. "Now where's the body?"

The priest unlocked the tall doors. Inside he led the policemen to the altar of the Madonna where Signora Di Giuseppi sat quietly in a pew.

"The Signora is very old. Ninety. But she wanted to wait until the police came. She wants to tell you what happened."

"What happened?" Welch asked.

"As far as I know, she was praying when she found the body."

"That's it?" Rodriguez said in disbelief.

"Apparently," the priest said.

"Father, when is the church open?" Welch asked.

"Nowadays we keep the church locked because too many precious altar ornaments have disappeared. Today we opened the doors at ten A.M. because we had a funeral mass scheduled." He shook his head. "We canceled it. The family is very upset, but I knew you wouldn't want anything touched."

Welch knelt to examine the corpse. He placed his hand inside the dead man's jacket. In an inside pocket he found a wallet. When he opened it, he whistled.

"What's up, Joe?" Rodriguez asked.

"He's a cop."

"No."

Welch looked at the face on the corpse. He was from a family of policemen and knew many of Manhattan's blue uniforms.

"His face is a mess. If he's George Giotti, he's retired. My dad used to work with him."

"That assistant district attorney? The one who was beaten? Are they related?" Rodriguez quizzed Welch.

"He's her father. The media will love this. Let's phone it in. Father," Welch turned to the priest, "we have to keep the premises clear until our investigation team completes its work."

"Anything you need," the priest agreed.

"The whole place must be sealed. You'll have to cancel all church activities."

The priest nodded.

"Is there someone who can escort the Signora home?" Welch asked.

The tired old woman had nodded in agreement when the priest repeated what she'd told him.

"I'll ask Father John."

"Father, please ask her not to speak to the media. Can you do that?"

"Of course."

"Fine. I'll leave Officer Rodriguez here while I call this in."

"Joe," Rodriguez said quietly. "Look at this."

Welch joined his partner at the far end of the altar where a gun lay.

"Murder weapon?" Rodriguez noted.

"I doubt it. The Mafia never leaves evidence. It probably belonged to Giotti."

"Then Giotti was armed."

"Seems so," Welch said.

❦ *Chapter 19* ❦

Vicki sat in her hospital bed, files strewn over it. She had convinced the doctor that she could work while recuperating. But she couldn't focus on her cases. Instead, she focused only on the doctor's words.

"*You are pregnant.*"

A wonderful flush surged through her when he said the words. She wanted to dance around the room, but her body was too sore. Instead she giggled. Feeling silly, she controlled herself.

"Please keep this confidential," she said matter-of-factly. "I'm not married."

"Did you plan for this?" Doctor Broan asked.

"Yes. I want a baby very much."

"Do you intend to marry?"

"No."

"Is the father known to you?"

"No," Vicki lied.

She wanted only her name on the birth certificate.

"When can I go home?" she asked.

"Depends upon how fast you heal."

Her face broke into a sad expression. The doctor saw the same look of experienced weariness on faces of battered wives. Women who were infrequently abused wore a look of anger on their faces. Constant batterings left looks of defeat.

That's how his patient looked. He had already guessed that she had been an abused child.

Vicki was napping when Policemen Joe Welch and Larry Rodriguez, accompanied by Vito Marchese, entered the hospital room. When she opened her eyes and saw Vito she smiled. Then she saw the two policemen.

"Did you find the wiseguys who beat me up?" she asked with professional poise.

"This isn't about that," Welch said.

Vito took her hand.

"We've sad news for you," he said.

"What's wrong?"

"Ms. Giotti, your father was murdered," Welch announced.

Her eyelids fluttered as if she could not tolerate this information. Her face contorted into a strange shape. She bit her lips. Still swollen, they bled. Vito reached for a tissue and handed it to her, but she waved it away.

"Who murdered him?" she asked.

"We think it was a Mafia hit," Rodriguez said, watching her carefully.

"Do you know anything about this, Ms. Giotti?" Welch asked.

Her heart pounded. She thought, thank God the bastard is dead, and I won't have to sit through another dinner where he says he loves me and denies the beatings.

But another part of her mourned.

"My father hasn't come to the hospital," she said softly. "My aunts told me he wasn't feeling well."

"When was the last time you saw him?"

"Before the kidnapping. We had dinner."

That night he'd looked beaten and said perhaps he couldn't live without the sauce. Vicki reminded him of their bargain. If he wanted to see her, he must attend AA.

Vito watched Vicki closely. He knew she prided herself on always being in control. He also knew that the policemen would notice that she hadn't cried.

"They weren't close," he said to the policemen, hoping that they believed him.

Welch wrote something in his notebook.

"Do you think his death is connected in any way to your kidnapping and assault?" he asked Vicki.

"I don't know."

"Did your father know Tony Tucci?" Rodriguez asked.

"You're assuming that Tucci was behind Vicki's assault?" Vito asked.

"We're simply asking questions," Welch said.

"I'm sure he knew about Tucci, but whether he knew him personally I really don't know," Vicki answered.

"Ms. Giotti, if you think of anything, would you call us?" Welch said.

"Of course."

They left quickly.

"Do you want me to stay?" Vito asked.

"Don't worry about me," she said abruptly. "I can handle this."

After Vito left she thought about her father's death. It probably had something to do with the assault she'd endured. Her office would investigate the matter but wouldn't allow her to be involved. But she must investigate her father's murder. She had to—for peace of mind.

In the circumstances, she decided this was a perfect time to take a leave of absence. She planned to do this so that she could have her baby with complete privacy. Why couldn't she investigate her father's death while nurturing her baby?

Later her aunts arrived, crying hysterically and wringing their hands. When they calmed down they told her about the funeral. They wondered whether Vicki would be well enough to leave the hospital to attend.

Vicki didn't answer their questions. Instead she asked her aunts for information.

"Aunt Tillie," Vicki said, "did Dad know Tony Tucci?"

Her aunts exchanged a look of apprehension. Both looked intensely distressed at her question.

"Why are you asking this?" Aunt Anna asked.

"The police think there might be a connection."

"Your father was a tortured man, Vicki darling," Aunt Tillie said sadly. "That's why he did all those . . ." she stumbled over the unmentionable words . . . "unfortunate things. He had lots of bad experiences when you were only a baby. Things that he never got over . . ."

"What things?" Vicki asked.

First they exchanged frightened looks, then they nodded to each other, and a stern look appeared on their faces, a sign of an established agreement to reveal nothing.

"Come on, you can tell me. He's dead," Vicki said bluntly.

"What did you want to know?" Aunt Tillie said.

"Did Dad know Tony Tucci?"

"I think so."

"Were they friends?"

"No."

"What was their relationship?"

"They both knew someone. . . ." She coughed on the words. Anna shook her head nervously, wordlessly pleading for Tillie to stop speaking. An expression of denial appeared on Tillie's face.

"You must tell me what you know," Vicki insisted. "Don't you want Dad's killer found?"

"But . . ."

"Please, Aunt Tillie!"

Vicki's anguish was painful for them to witness. They had passively endured her violent childhood, watching her pain, too frightened to protect her.

Suddenly one of them felt too guilty to go on being silent.

"I can't tell you very much," Aunt Anna said breathlessly. "All I can tell you is that your father and Tony Tucci were once in love with the same woman."

PART IV

NEW YORK CITY

——————1952——————

FRANCESCA

❧ *Chapter 20* ❧

*L*isten, you're nothing. Do you hear me?" Tony shouted to the man held by his two bodyguards. Imitating his hero, Edward G. Robinson, Joey Morro stared back at Tony with defiance.

"You've got the whole situation ass backwards," Joey complained. "I didn't talk to the cops. That's a bullshit story you've been given by the guys who want to break you down. And you're falling for it, dope. The way they're going to do you in is to get rid of all your old *goombahs*. Like me."

Joey chafed under the stranglehold of the two thick-armed men who held him.

Tony walked over to the captive man. Slowly he removed his hand from the pocket of his beige shark-skin jacket. His sapphire ring glinted in the semidarkness as he smacked Joey on the right cheek. Without a second's hesitation he slapped the man on the left cheek.

It took a few minutes for Joey to catch his breath. He stared defiantly at Tony.

"Okay. Okay. You're sore because I didn't check with you before I did the hit. You don't talk to people about your work, and I don't either. I had a job to do, and I did it."

"You're supposed to be my lieutenant, Joey," Tony said harshly. "Remember? I'm the boss."

Joey measured his next words carefully.

"Don Allegro is the boss. Remember? I'm working for him. You're working for him. Am I right?"

"You work for me. Understand?" Tony replied angrily.

Joey pondered his words. During his silence the two captors held him fast, bending his shoulders, which caused him extreme pain.

"Tell these guys to bug off," he said.

"First tell me the whole story," Tony ordered.

"Okay. Okay. It was like this. The Don told me to hit Braso fast. I asked him if I should report to you, and he said no, that this was a direct order from him and it had to be kept secret. I told him that you wouldn't like it, and the Don said, 'That's okay, tell Tony to talk to me.' " Joey paused. "The thing is, Tony, the hit gave Carmine the advantage, not you. Braso was moving into his Brooklyn territory. I didn't tell you because I knew you'd go nuts. So I did the hit and went home. That's when your guys grabbed me. But," he said, with lips tightly drawn, "I was going to tell you about it. Honest. Look, if there's a war, you can count on me."

"Oh, sure." Tony laughed, hitting the side of his chest, then folding his arms in a Napoleonic pose.

"Boss, I can't change the rules. Carmine's ambitious. He wants to make his bones."

"He made his bones. Now he wants the whole pie."

"And there's no one to stop him except you. That's why Carmine hates you. Everybody knows that the Don chose you to succeed him. There's no doubt about that, is there?"

"Then why is he hiding things from me?"

"Tony, he'd cut my fingers off if he knew I told you about Braso. But you're my guy. You've always been."

Joey checked Tony's somber expression, knew it conveyed that he was still in trouble. Joey knew Tony well. They'd grown up on Sullivan Street. When they were young Joey had always fought for Tony. When they became professionals, he was Tony's lieutenant. But when the Don asked him to whack someone and not tell Tony, he couldn't refuse. After all, the Don was the boss of all bosses, the Godfather.

"Look, Joey, you're telling me that if the Don tells you something, you do it, without consulting me? Well, if you could do that, then we could go out and eat pasta and you could pull a .45 and kill me, too. Tell me, am I right?"

"Hey, Tony. You're my best friend. Everybody knows that."

"That's the reason you might get close to me. You see, this is the way it goes. If you do one thing for the Don without telling me, that means he's setting you up for something big. I couldn't care less that you bopped Braso. He was an asshole. What I care about is that you didn't discuss it with me. So what's the next step, huh? You going to rub me out?"

Tony put his hand on Joey's chin and squeezed it until Joey grimaced. Joey knew Tony was making sense. He'd been set up, and by the main man himself: the Godfather, Don Allegro.

"I'm sorry, Tony. I didn't think."

"Remember what I used to tell you when we were kids? I'll do the thinking for both of us. You couldn't get to first base without me. What happened to make you forget that?"

Joey looked down at the ground. His round brown eyes conveyed regret and shame.

"I don't know. The Don was very specific that I shouldn't tell you. I didn't know what to do."

"Maybe you were flattered by the old man taking a shine to you." Tony's eyes glinted with anger. "Maybe you thought, I'm going to come up in the world, and I don't need my buddy anymore. Is that it?"

Playfully, Tony slapped Joey on the chin a couple of times. Then he gestured to the bodyguards to let the captive go. When they released him Joey brightened up.

"You're not mad anymore?"

"I'm stinking mad."

Tony signaled his men that he wanted Joey to remember this lesson. He walked out of the room and waited in an outer office while his men did his bidding.

Tony constantly scrutinized the behavior of his business associates. In business Tony was wily, artful, and cunning. To Tony, being one step ahead of everyone else was essential. He watched everyone carefully.

Even the Don's orders, though obeyed at once, were constantly examined.

Like this new situation. What did the Don want? He told everyone Tony was like his son. Then why did he ask Joey to do the Braso hit without telling Tony?

Tony's rules were never to repeat mistakes and always to look for betrayal. He knew there would be serious consequences to what had happened. This was more than a breach of friendship. The facts revealed that the Don was constructing an elaborate system of treachery.

Something had changed.

What could have upset Don Allegro? When he had married Francesca the Don expressed his disappointment because Tony didn't marry his sister, Sally. Was that enough to garner the old man's fury?

Suddenly, Tony knew.

Sally Allegro always had the hots for Tony. He treated her with kid gloves, conveying that she was a lady who shouldn't be touched. While this was meant as a compliment, Sally took it as an insult. Could she have influenced her brother to believe that Tony wasn't to be trusted any longer?

Something was missing. Joey could find out what it was. But first Joey needed to learn his lesson.

Tony's men worked quickly. Inside the room Mike the Crab grabbed hold of Joey's right wrist. With a quick twist he sprained it. Joey screamed. His hand hung loosely from the rest of his arm, and he couldn't feel his fingers. Instead of backing away, Joey elbowed Mike to gain time. This gesture angered Mike. Savagely, he grabbed Joey's outstretched arm in a paralyzing hold. Two seconds later Joey's arm was pulled out of its socket.

On the other side of Joey, Benny the Pill came down on Joey's left shoulder. He slammed a thick fist into it, digging for a nerve juncture. Suddenly Joey's head jerked spastically. Against his better judgment he tried to break free, but Benny slammed his fist into Joey's face. Cursing, Joey spit blood, realizing that he was in danger.

Instead of defending himself, Joey rocked unsteadily as excruciating pain soared through his body. He took a couple of deep breaths, closed his eyes, and dug the heels of his shoes deep into the floor, waiting for the end.

But he was lucky. Tony appeared. Joey knew the worst was over because Tony didn't like to watch men die.

"Okay, Joey, here's what I want you to do. After you get your body fixed up I want you to find out what the hell is going on between Carmine and the Don. Understand?"

Joey looked up at Tony. Wordlessly, he shook his head.

"Because, pal, if you don't come up with something, Mike and Benny won't stop with your arms. Next time they'll break your legs. Then you'll have a hard time humping your ladies, won't you, Joey, baby?" Tony threatened.

He walked out of the room. When he left the building his car was waiting. Once he was inside, Tony's spirits fell. He might have to sentence his best friend to death.

❧ *Chapter 21* ❧

*F*rancesca snuggled deep inside her pyramid mink coat. With its natural shoulders, small collar, and turned-back cocktail cuffs, it was the latest look from the Bergdorf Goodman fur salon. Francesca's slim hand caressed the soft skins, a new mutation named "Sapphire": clear, light blue skins that cost $36,000. Tony had bought the coat to celebrate the birth of their baby, Arianna.

For months they fussed about the baby's name and settled on Arianna because Francesca said it sounded like the name of a goddess. She read mythology books and thought gods and goddesses were inspirational. Their stories of performing amazing feats while being threatened and pursued by enemies of tremendous strength thrilled her.

Francesca liked courage; it was one of the reasons she loved Tony.

Francesca brushed her lips against Tony's cheek. They were at the Chez Bon, a nightclub on East Forty-eighth Street that resembled ancient Rome. Stylized versions of arches and centurions cast long shadows upon the crowd while Mitch Miller played "My Heart Cries for You." The song was number three on the hit parade and one of Tony's favorites.

A large painting entitled *Neptune* hung behind a long bar on one side of the room. It featured a small aquarium of unusual fish painted in the style of Rousseau. This painting, contrasted against the Roman look, gave a dizzying effect to the club.

The bar was very modern—bright pink leather with matching plush leather bar stools. On each table, pink was the main color: pink flowers, a pink marble table-top, and pink satin chairs.

"Honey, I love you," Tony whispered.

Francesca's green eyes sparkled at his display of love. Since Arianna's birth Francesca had noticed a change in Tony. He fussed over their daughter. Was her crib comfortable? How about her diapers? And her food? She was his princess, and he wasn't interested in anyone else. Even Francesca.

Francesca felt hurt and talked to Antoinette Tucci.

"She's Tony's first child. He's completely taken with her," Antoinette said.

"What should I do?"

"Francesca, Tony adores you, but you're the mother of his daughter."

"I'm a woman."

"A very young woman," Antoinette said, shaking her head.

"Tony's father was the same way. After I had children our love was no longer passionate."

"Were you happy?" Francesca asked the stern-faced woman.

"Women get happiness from children. We love our husbands, but the sweetheart part is over. It's better this way. Life is hard. A woman needs strength to give her family the best chances."

Francesca also spoke to her mother, Matilda, who confirmed Antoinette's view of marriage. When Francesca spoke to Jamie, Jamie said that both women were crazy.

"Sexual passion continues until you die, Francesca. The fact that you have a child doesn't mean shit."

Francesca winced. She hated Jamie's cursing.

"Jamie, please."

"All right, but you know what I mean. Married couples like sex. Why should they give it up?"

But Francesca had a problem because Tony rarely made love to her. Often it happened after a night out, like tonight.

In anticipation Francesca had carefully combed her Italian haircut so the short, layered locks with the casual wisps caused her red hair to look like a regal crown. She wore a form-fitting evening skirt of dark green satin. Above it was a daring blouse with balloon sleeves and a plunging neckline. The outfit set off her exquisite pearls.

Francesca chose an elegant green silk bra and panty set to wear underneath. A matching garter belt held up the silk stockings covering her legs. Her shoes had jeweled heals that matched the ornate blouse.

When she leaned forward her breasts brushed against Tony's hand. He kissed her on the ear.

"Happy?" he asked.

"I'll be happier when we go home."

He was pleased at her answer. Generally he didn't visit clubs with Francesca, because it was business. But tonight was her eighteenth birthday, and he wanted to shower her with attention.

But the difficulties with Carmine Solari haunted him. Tony couldn't relax even when he was home. At least he was sure that his family was not in danger, because the Mafia did not involve women and children in their arguments.

Still, he didn't like to appear in public with Francesca, in case there was an accident. If someone tried to shoot him, she might accidentally be hurt.

At home Tony focused on Arianna. The baby mesmerized him. All the previous love Tony had experienced was surpassed by this enormous passion for his daughter. She was everything to him—so much so that he neglected Francesca and could see that she was unhappy. He tried to replace his passion with gifts. And, on nights like tonight, he made love to her.

He knew she wanted him. He put his hand underneath her skirt and fondled the inner part of her thighs. She squeezed his arm. Tony kissed her.

Suddenly there was a roar of gunshots. His bodyguards jumped on Tony and Francesca, pinning them under the table. At the entrance two men shot at them, but Tony had taken the precaution of stationing several bodyguards at the bar. In one second their guns were drawn, and the two assassins were blown against the wall, their blood mixing with the Roman motif. The place looked like a Roman circus.

Underneath her husband's body Francesca's face was smashed against the floor. Her skirt and blouse were torn, revealing an ample show of flesh.

"Are you all right, darling?" Tony asked.

"No," she said.

Quickly Tony put his jacket around Francesca.

"Let's get out of here," he said.

His men escorted them to a waiting car. The car sped away, heading downtown.

Tony examined Francesca's face and saw there were scratches on it.

"That's why I don't like to take you out. You could have been hurt."

"Stop treating me like a child. Who were those men? Why did they try to kill you, Tony?"

"That's none of your business, Francesca."

"Tony, tell me why this happened."

"No, Francesca. But I promise you it will never happen again."

She turned away from him. Underneath her anger was a gnawing sensation. If Tony was a legal business-man, why were men shooting at him?

Had he lied to her?

And what else had he lied about?

❧ *Chapter 22* ❧

Okay, this is the story. Carmine Solari married Sally Allegro in Las Vegas over the weekend.''

At the other end of the phone, Tony's fists clenched when he heard Joey's message.

"Tony, maybe that's why the Don has changed. Have you talked to him?"

"I've stayed away from the compound. No sense in asking for trouble. Where did you get this information?"

"Everyone on the street knows things before us. What do you want me to do?"

"We're going to have to break bones," Tony said.

"But the Feds are watching us like hawks."

"It doesn't matter, because I'm going to be in the public eye anyway when things go down."

"What do we do?"

"Meet me tonight at Aldo's."

Tony hung up the phone, left the bedroom, and went into the kitchen. Francesca was out with the baby. A pot of coffee was on the stove. He turned on the flame under the pot, took a slice of Wonder Bread from a package on the counter, and put it into the gleaming toaster. He opened a cupboard. A set of very white dinnerware was stacked efficiently. He took out a cup and saucer. The coffee began perking, and Tony turned off the flame. He poured the coffee into the cup. He picked up the toast and sat at the table. Everything in the kitchen was cheerful, but he did not feel happy.

What to do about the Don? The old man was being manipulated by Carmine because of his marriage to Sally. There was nothing more important to an Italian than a relative. Though Tony was indispensable to the Don, Carmine was now a brother-in-law.

There was only one way out of this. He had to remove the Don. But how? The old man never left the compound except for a funeral or a wedding.

Tony had an idea. Arianna must be baptized. The Don would attend the ceremony. If he didn't, it would be an open insult to Tony.

But how to hit him?

Suppose the hit was committed by someone no one could suspect was tied to Tony. There was one man who qualified. Giotti. Everyone knew that Giotti hated Tony's guts.

That was it. He had to set up Giotti. What could pull the strings to make Giotti act? Giotti was an honest cop who didn't take bribes. The only thing that could upset Giotti was someone close to his heart.

Victoria Regina! That was the way to Giotti. Tony

could use Francesca to accomplish his scheme. She was a perfect choice.

Francesca wheeled the baby carriage into the lobby of the Fifth Avenue building. The doorman tipped his hat, opened the door for her, and helped her with the enormous carriage. In the carriage Arianna was sleeping. At six months old, Arianna looked like a Botticelli angel. Wisps of golden blond hair covered her perfectly shaped head. Her beautiful blue eyes were like the heavens above. Her delicate lips curled happily as she slept. Her tiny body was in a lovely pink cotton suit Francesca had purchased at Best and Company. Matilda said it was frivolous to shop at the elegant Fifth Avenue store, but Francesca laughed at her mother, reminding her that Tony wanted only the best for Arianna.

In the elevator she hummed to her baby. In the past weeks she had prayed to God that Arianna would always be happy. She'd be a good wife so that Arianna could have everything a child needed—money, and two parents who adored her.

She'd failed her first child, Victoria Regina. But God had given her a second chance, and she was determined not to fail. Whatever it took, she would protect Arianna.

When she reached the apartment Francesca smoothed down her pencil-slim skirt. She wore a navy blue suit. The silk-lined skirt was very chic and rustled when she moved. It was topped with a hip-hugger cardigan jacket from Lord and Taylor. Under the jacket Francesca wore a silk jersey sweater of teal blue, accented by diamond earrings and rings.

When Tony heard the buzzer he waited in the foyer while his bodyguards opened the door. When he saw his wife he rushed to her side.

"Francesca, darling, I've good news. I've planned our angel's baptism. We'll do it at St. Anthony's right away."

Francesca noticed that Tony's bodyguards were apprehensive as he picked up his daughter. Had something happened? When Arianna saw her father she smiled, but Francesca couldn't relax.

"A perfect baby, thanks to you," Tony said.

He put his hand under Francesca's chin and kissed her. She tried not to stiffen under his touch, but she couldn't stifle her feelings. He looked at her sharply.

"Put the baby down for a nap, Francesca," Tony said in a serious tone of voice.

"What's wrong?"

"We'll talk when the baby is asleep."

In the bedroom Francesca tended to Arianna's needs. She undressed her, changed her diaper, put on a little shirt, and placed her in the crib. She hummed a lullaby till the baby fell asleep. Then she walked into the kitchen, where Tony was drinking coffee.

"You look sexy for the middle of the afternoon," he said, winking at her.

"Thank you," she said with modesty.

"I have something to talk to you about," he said gravely.

"What's wrong?"

"It's about Victoria Regina," he said.

"Has George hurt her?"

"No. But I've received information that George is

annoying the Don. He keeps asking questions about the Don's people."

"But he hates you, not Don Allegro."

"He hates anyone with money and power because he has none."

"How does this affect Victoria Regina?"

"She's in danger. There are people who want to impress the Don, and they will do anything."

"Like what?"

"I'm not sure. They feel Giotti is a pest. You must tell him to take Victoria Regina away until this whole mess blows over."

"Will he believe me?"

"Giotti will believe you. He knows you love your daughter."

Chapter 23

*F*rancesca walked down Eleventh Street, tugging nervously at the belt of her wraparound coat. It was white and expensive and was the only garment in her wardrobe casual enough not to irritate George. Underneath the coat she wore a white angora sweater over a tweed skirt that hugged her slim hips, then flared into permanent pleats. Her brown pigskin gloves matched her shoulder bag.

She had worked on the outfit for hours. She wanted to look as casual as possible, so that George wouldn't be upset by a display of wealth. However, she couldn't resist wearing her diamond earrings and wedding ring because part of her wanted to show George that she had moved up in the world.

She shivered as she approached Hudson Street, not from the weather but from the memory of her life on this corner. She passed the tenement where she had lived with George and where her darling daughter still lived. She looked up to the fourth floor and wondered what would happen if she entered the building, rang a neighbor's bell, and climbed the four flights to the apartment where she'd lived with George and Victoria Regina. She'd knock on the door, and perhaps Victoria Regina would answer. Her daughter was two, and whenever Francesca saw her in the park Victoria Regina was clean and well-dressed. She looked like a healthy little girl, except for the fact that occasionally she had black-and-blue marks on her legs and arms.

Nervously, Francesca adjusted the sunglasses she wore. They were the expensive, slanted type that movie stars wore. She had ordered seven pair in various colors at Bergdorf Goodman. Today she wore black.

Francesca headed for the Hudson Street Tavern. In the past the bar had been a hangout for policemen. These days the bar was a mixture of working-class men, policemen, poets, writers, actors, and filmmakers.

Jamie had given Francesca this information, so once inside Francesca wasn't surprised at the lineup of sturdy men dressed in dungarees and shirts on one side of the bar. On the other side were women in black leather skirts and men in black corduroy pants, the current outfit for the artistic set.

Jamie had offered to accompany her to the tavern, but Francesca knew that George would react badly, and the purpose of her visit might be ruined. This was something she must do alone. She didn't know that two bodyguards were shadowing her to make certain nothing would happen.

Francesca drew in a sharp breath when the smoke filled her nostrils. She coughed. Several men looked in her direction, displaying an immediate interest in the attractive eighteen-year-old.

At the end of the bar George Giotti was watching Kurt flip a hamburger. The tavern specialized in knockwurst and hamburgers. Patrons loved the black bread and strong mustard that accompanied these snacks.

George's mouth watered because he hadn't eaten lunch. He was drinking too much and, as a safeguard, always ate a hamburger at five o'clock. He was so intent on watching Kurt that he didn't see Francesca.

When his buddy Otto whistled and whispered, "That's some lady," George looked up. With a start he realized that the lovely redhead was his former wife.

He walked quickly over to her and grabbed her arm.

"What the hell are you doing here?" he demanded.

Francesca looked into the handsome face of her ex-husband.

"I must talk to you, George. It's urgent."

"What the hell do you want? Don't ask to see Vicki. She thinks you're dead."

"Oh, no, you didn't—you couldn't—"

"It's the best way. I don't want my little girl finding out her mother is a dirty whore married to a killer."

Several artists looked up. One of them walked over to Francesca.

"Do you need help, ma'am?" he asked.

George glared at the man. "She's fine," he said.

"I'm asking the lady."

Francesca shook her head weakly. Her strength left her body as if George had dealt her a physical blow.

"Victoria Regina is in danger."

"What's this about?"

"It's about the Don. There are men who want to impress him. They know he's annoyed at you because you keep sticking your nose into his business."

"And into your hubby's business."

"Tony is trying to help."

"Your husband's business is harming people. Don't you know that?"

Francesca shook her head violently, though her heart was heavy.

"Tony wants to save Victoria Regina," she insisted.

"You're a fool," George said.

"He says they'll hurt Victoria Regina to get at you. Tony says you must take her out of town."

"Tony? Why should I believe that son of a bitch? He's one of them. This is probably his idea."

"Tony would never do anything to harm Victoria Regina. He knows I'd leave him if he did. Don't you see? He's trying to help. George, listen to me. You must protect Victoria Regina. Promise me you will."

❧ *Chapter 24* ❧

St. Anthony's Church was decked out for Christmas festivities. The holly and ivy, traditional in America, were missing. Instead the altars held startling red carnations, and on the green marble pillars, fern wreaths were decoratively tied with bright red ribbons.

It was four days before Christmas and the morning of Arianna's baptism. Tony Tucci worried about security and requested that the church doors be locked.

At first Father Mike was reluctant for worshipers were welcome in the church anytime. Tony explained that one of the guests, Don Allegro, had enemies. To avoid trouble, the priest agreed to lock the church's doors.

The baptism party used only the rear doors Father Mike left open for the Tucci guests.

During the ceremony Arianna cried. She kept trying to remove her bonnet. Her godmother, Ellen Tucci, held the screaming child. Francesca comforted the baby but knew that Arianna's temper was not easily soothed.

"Sweetheart," Francesca whispered, "it'll soon be over."

The baptism was conducted at a small altar on the left side of the church. Eleven people attended the ceremony: the screaming baby, the parents, the godparents, Don Allegro, the four bodyguards, and Father Mike. Antoinette Tucci, the baby's only living grandparent, was ill with the flu. Francesca's parents had been killed in a subway accident.

Arianna's wails caused confusion as the priest spoke the holy words. None of the four bodyguards could hear the sounds coming from the rear of the church.

From his hiding place, George Giotti concentrated on the bodyguards. Both sides of his head were pounding. He'd been crazed since Francesca had warned him that Vicki was in danger. He had to act quickly against the Don. But how? The Don rarely left his compound. When his sister told him Arianna was to be baptized, he realized this was a golden opportunity, knowing the Don would attend.

On the morning of the baptism George chose a fortyfive from his gun collection, donned a bullet-proof vest, and left to perform his duty.

George crept slowly, hiding behind pillars as the priest poured water over the baby's head and Arianna's screams grew louder.

Big Philly, the Don's bodyguard, spotted a shadow and turned quickly.

The Don came to attention.

"What's wrong?" he asked.

Philly motioned to his right.

"Who's there?" he called.

Tony saw George Giotti's angry face and knew his plan was working. He motioned to his bodyguards to do nothing.

George walked carefully over to the baptismal altar. His uniform shone in the morning sunlight.

"This is nice," he said angrily. "Father Mike, why are these killers in your church?"

The priest answered calmly, "A baby is being baptized. It's my duty to perform the ceremony. What can I do for you, officer?"

"I think these men are armed, Father. I'd like to check them out. Do you mind?"

"If you think it's necessary," he said nervously.

Francesca took Arianna from her sister-in-law's arms. She almost shouted George's name when she saw him, but Tony grasped her arm. She knew there was going to be trouble. She walked slowly to the rear of the church holding her baby in her arms.

George stared at Francesca with an evil look on his face.

"I see you also let a whore into church," he said angrily.

Hearing this insult, the Don gasped. He glanced quickly at Tony, wondering why he didn't act. He decided it was because Arianna and Francesca were present. But the Don was not inhibited by them. Something must be done.

Don Allegro turned toward George, pretending he did not recognize him.

"Officer, is this the way you speak to a mother?"

"She's a whore," George snarled.

Francesca was petrified. Shaking, she knelt before the statue of the Madonna and Child. "Please save my baby," she prayed.

With a slight nod Don Allegro ordered his bodyguards to remove Giotti from the church. As the bodyguards walked toward George he watched them carefully. He must get them to draw first or his plan would fail.

"Dirty dagos," he cursed.

Big Philly yelped and pulled out a gun from his jacket pocket. The Don's other bodyguard, Louis the Lip, backed Philly's action. Quickly, George pulled out his gun. The first slug hit Big Philly in the middle of his forehead. Ellen Tucci screamed as George shot Louie the Lip in the stomach. Then, watching Tony, George aimed at the Don.

By now the Don realized this was a setup because Tony didn't act. His heart beat rapidly. In his left-hand pocket he carried a pillbox from Florence, Italy. When he reached for it, George fired. The Don emitted a loud scream and fell at the foot of the altar.

George aimed his gun at Tony.

"I'm not armed," Tony said, raising his hands in the air. "And neither are they." He motioned to his men. "You'd better find out whether I'm telling the truth, because if you shoot an unarmed man, that's murder, isn't it? Giotti, you're in enough trouble. The Don wasn't carrying a gun."

George gestured to the priest.

"Father, would you search Mr. Allegro?"

Nervously, the priest followed George's orders. He looked shaken as he said, "He's not armed."

George shrugged his shoulders.

"Well, it looked as if he was reaching for a gun. Search Tucci, Father. And those guys."

George motioned to Tony's bodyguards. The priest fumbled nervously as he carried out George's request. When he was finished he shook his head.

"They're not armed. Please, officer, this is horrible. These men . . ." he said sadly, "I have to give them the last rites."

"Go ahead, Father. But first call the precinct. Tell them that George Giotti has gunned down Don Allegro," George boasted.

"May I take my wife home?" Tony asked. "The baby is upset by all this bloodshed."

"If she's your daughter, she may as well get used to it," George snickered.

"Only animals hurt women and children," Tony said savagely.

George's eyes slanted in anger. His trigger finger itched, but he knew that, given the situation, he couldn't get away with killing Tony. "Get lost," he grumbled.

Tony signaled his men to follow him. In the rear of the church Francesca wept. "Are you hurt?" Tony asked. "Is Arianna hurt?"

But she could not answer him. Her sobs continued, upsetting Arianna.

"Let's leave this place. Your ex-husband is an animal," Tony said, trying to hide his satisfaction.

The headlines ran two to one in favor of Policeman George Giotti. What luck that he happened to be in church when armed mafiosi appeared. What could he do but defend himself when armed gangsters went after him? The detectives on the case realized that there were improprieties, but the police chief was pleased. When questioned by detectives, Tony Tucci said that it was an unfortunate incident. The Don was reaching for his medication, and Giotti thought he was armed. Other witnesses agreed. Father Mike, in the interest of keeping things low-key, said he'd been startled when the Don's bodyguards drew guns. He did not mention the angry insults that Giotti hurled at Mrs. Tucci. What was the point? The dead were dead, and the notoriety must be squashed. As a result of this whitewash, George Giotti was acclaimed a hero. And no one at the precinct realized that the fine hand of Tony Tucci was behind the Don's murder.

❧ *Chapter 25* ❧

Send Angelo Benedetti to see me," Tony said to his consigliere, Bustero Da Costa.

The gray-haired man nodded. He expected Tony to act accordingly, because there was going to be trouble. The council had ruled that Tony was the acting head of the Allegro family. Because Carmine was married to Sally Allegro, he'd protested the council's ruling.

The Don's widow pleaded with Tony not to cause more bloodshed.

"Tony, please do not kill the father of Sally's future children."

"Signora, I will never hurt the family," Tony vowed.

As he lied Tony pondered what scenario could be created to satisfy both his need to eliminate Carmine and the Allegro family's need to believe it was not Tony's doing.

He held the Signora's hand.

"When there is this kind of disharmony, I cannot answer for Carmine's safety. He must put himself under my protection."

"I've tried to talk to him."

Her weary eyes, exhausted from crying for her late husband, were filled with anguish. Her pain was all-consuming. She had loved her husband for fifty years and did not know whether she could go on without him.

Because Tony was like him, the Don had taken him under his wing. He said to his wife: "Tony is like our son. He treats us with respect. He adores his mother. And he is tough in business."

When Tony married Francesca instead of Sally Allegro, the Don's feelings were hurt. When Arianna was born he said, "She could have been my blood."

He never liked Francesca. Signora Allegro recognized the denial in Francesca's eyes and understood it.

If a Mafia wife accepted reality, could she live with her husband, cook for him, and give him her body to love? It would not be possible for a woman to pray to God one minute and love a killer the next.

The Signora wondered how Francesca felt after seeing the blood spilled at her child's baptism. How would Francesca cope with this terrible reality?

"Jamie, I must get away from Tony. Will you help me?" Francesca pleaded.

"But you love Tony, don't you?"

"Yes, but I can't live with him any longer for the baby's sake. I don't want her to grow up around bullets and blood. I want her to have a decent life, not like"—her voice caught—"like Victoria Regina."

"Do you have a plan?"

"I must find a place where Tony won't find us," Francesca said. "If I change my name and lead a quiet life somewhere far away, he won't be able to trace me, will he?"

"How about California?"

"I don't know anyone there."

"Don't worry, Francesca. We'll find a way," Jamie said.

Angelo Benedetti watched the two large men getting out of the car. One of them was Carmine Solari. He'd been a Golden Gloves champ when he was young, and his body reflected a superb muscular development. Every day he worked out at Eddie's Gym on Third Avenue. He liked to get there about three in the afternoon, work till six, shower, dress, and walk around the corner to where one of his mistresses, Franny Terco, lived. Carmine fucked her for a couple of hours, then headed home to eat dinner with Sally. After he spent a couple of hours with his wife he'd appear at a local nightclub. There he'd meet another woman, or perhaps two. Carmine conducted business with his cronics while fondling his women under the table. After the club closed he'd take his women to his Waldorf suite and bang them until the sun rose. Routinely, he'd dress and return home to sleep until mid-afternoon.

This was the typical life of a mafioso, except Carmine was legendary because he had the sexual appetite of an animal.

Older-generation mafiosi like Don Allegro treated mistresses like wives. The Don had a mistress for many years until she pleaded to marry because she wanted children. He gave permission, funded her husband's business, and treated her children with respect.

Don Allegro was aware of Carmine's love life as a single man. When he married Sally, the Don told Carmine to cut out his extracurricular activities. He knew his sister was violently jealous after seeing her rage when Tony married Francesca. There was no reason for Sally's reaction. Tony had never touched her. Still, Sally jealously shrieked that she'd been jilted by Tony.

Sally Allegro Solari was a woman who had kept her passion under wraps for too long. She wanted Tony and, as the only single woman in the Allegro family, thought she'd have him. The Don promised her. When he reneged, Sally's passion turned to hatred. For revenge she secretly eloped with Carmine, Tony's enemy.

Sally sowed the seeds of mistrust by telling the Don that Tony could no longer be trusted because Francesca did not accept her place in the Allegro family. Francesca was a woman who preferred to be American and acted as if she didn't belong to the Italian community. The women in the Allegro family did not like her. She was too proud and too regal. She could cause trouble.

The Don listened to his sister because she was recognized as having a man's mind and courage. This was why he'd wanted her to marry Tony, for Sally needed a strong man.

Carmine married Sally without particularly thinking

about her personality or her emotional needs. He simply viewed the marriage as an opportunity to link up with the Allegro clan and consolidate his strength against his rival, Tony Tucci.

After marriage Sally focused her sexual appetite on Carmine. The fact that he was an animal in bed delighted her. Sally and Carmine had two months of heavy sex before she realized she was not the only woman in his life. Someone began sending her photos of Carmine with other women.

At first she thought the photos were a setup job, but when she recognized the familiar nightclub settings, Sally realized that her oversexed husband was not only banging her but also spreading it around.

Sally went crazy. She asked her brother-in-law, Jim the Belly, to find out what was going on. Jim, whose fondness for belly dancers had earned him his name, empathized with Carmine. He warned Carmine that Sally knew too much. Pissed off, Carmine told his wife to butt out. His business outside of the house was not her affair.

But the photos kept arriving. Early one morning Sally decided to pay a visit to her husband's Waldorf suite. Before she left the house she put a gun in her purse. The Don had given it to her for protection. She had a permit and knew how to use it.

Sally entered the Waldorf, went into the elevator, and rode to the eleventh floor. Carmine's bodyguards were stationed outside the suite. When they saw the boss's wife, they tried to stop her.

"He's not here," Rocco Russo said, motioning for his buddy to warn Carmine that Sally was there.

"Get out of my way," Sally said in an ominous tone

of voice. They obeyed the late Don's sister and moved aside.

She walked into the luxurious suite. The parlor room was French Provincial, with gilded antique furniture, portraits of French royalty on the walls, and sofas of plush blue velvet. She admired the surroundings, swearing under her breath because Carmine had never taken her anywhere this luxurious.

She walked over to the double doors and quietly opened them. Behind them her husband was fucking two Harlem showgirls. They were gorgeous black women.

In shock, Sally watched as Carmine was in ecstasy. Leaning against a wall, he thrust with his pulsating penis, which gave the showgirl incredible energy. She brought her legs up around his neck and quivered as her body accepted his savage blows. He picked her up and walked over to the bed, where the other showgirl played with her breasts. As he thrust his penis into one woman, the other woman manipulated her waiting vagina, taunting Carmine. He opened his moist mouth and sucked her vagina. He rammed his cock into the woman beneath him while he rammed his tongue into the woman beside him. The body under him writhed with exquisite torture, and savage screams escaped her. Her arms and legs hugged Carmine's body as tightly as they could as he kept pumping her. Her hot pink lips shouted for more.

"Give me all you got," she screamed.

Her female friend was ready for more than Carmine's tongue. She put her tongue in Carmine's mouth and sucked on his. He gave a violent thrust to the woman beneath him and erupted. His shattering climax filled her with a flood of semen. Slowly she relaxed, making it easy for Carmine to slide right out of her vagina and into the next one.

He was hard immediately. He sucked on the woman's breasts, then on her nipples. He pumped the second woman with the same ferocity as he had the first. The second woman began a series of screams that conveyed her erotic pleasure. She bit her lips as her friend watched. Then the first woman jumped on Carmine's back to begin a fucking motion in the rear. Her vaginal area was incredibly excited, and rubbing against his anus sent her wild. She moaned with passion. Then the three figures on the bed swelled to a mountainous climax with a grunting series of screams.

Sally went crazy. She intended to scare her husband and order his women off the premises. But the sight of Carmine banging two women broke Sally's rationality.

She reached for the gun in her purse. Without hesitation, she squeezed the trigger. There was one loud bang. Two. Three. Then four.

Tony Tucci put the phone down. He placed his hand on his forehead, passed it gently to the right and the left, and closed his eyes. It was a bold plan, and it had worked. Angelo had followed Tony's orders perfectly. The photographs had stirred Sally's jealousy, and she lost control, as he knew she would.

Carmine hadn't thought ahead when he married Sally. He wanted the Allegro family connection and assumed that Sally would be like other wives: respectful, a good cook, and a good lay, without asking too many questions.

Tony took advantage of Carmine's stupidity. He'd formulated an expertly crafted plan, and it had worked.

Now no one in the Allegro family could blame Tony for the demise of Carmine Solari.

Chapter 26

*T*he Village Café was noisy, and Jamie was in a bad mood. She should have been pleased that Francesca finally realized her sweet-talking, passionate husband was a hood. Jamie had wanted to point this out to Francesca but didn't, because she couldn't destroy Francesca's deep belief in love, marriage, and children.

In contrast, Jamie shared none of those values. Dressed in the black leather garb and the ostentatious makeup, being sexually direct was her way of showing her own values. She thought most women's lives were dishonest, so rebellion was Jamie's preference.

She was angry tonight. Her publisher was destroying her book. She'd consulted a lawyer who said she could take the book away from them.

A true rebel would, but Jamie didn't.

She wanted the fame of publication, wanted the world to know the two women in the book.

Francesca was the more courageous of the two. She believed in love.

Jamie did not.

Jamie sat at the bar with a foul expression on her face. Her friends came here to laugh, to smoke, to drink, to find sex partners, and to avoid unhappiness. She sat at the bar for hours, drinking martinis. Slobbering drunk, she talked to the bartender, an Italian named Pete.

"Hey, Pete, want to go home with me?" she stammered.

Pete tolerantly motioned to cut her off.

"I think you've had enough, Jamie. Why don't you go home?"

"I haven't had enough, but my friend Francesca has," Jamie sputtered. "She's leaving Tough Tony. What do you think of that?"

Pete didn't bat an eyelash as he motioned to one of the other bartenders to cover his end of the bar. Quickly, he went to the back office and phoned in this information to his bookie, knowing that Tucci would hear about it soon.

Francesca had planned her escape for days, and now that it was time she kept running to the bathroom. The thought of leaving Victoria Regina almost caused her to cancel her escape. Jamie thought that maybe, after Francesca left Tony, the courts would be kinder to her. As soon as Arianna was safely hidden, Francesca could return to fight George for Victoria Regina.

Now she must save Arianna. Jamie was going to

meet her at the airport with a bag filled with Arianna's clothes, and cash. Francesca already had her ticket, paid for out of housekeeping money.

It was time. Francesca told Tony that she was taking Arianna for a stroll. She walked up to Twelfth Street and hailed a cab.

"Hey, lady, I can't fit that carriage into this cab," the driver said.

"Don't worry. I'm leaving it. Please take me to La Guardia Airport."

When they arrived Francesca went to the airlines desk. The clerk thought Francesca's nervousness came from traveling with a baby.

"Don't worry," the clerk said. "Many mothers travel, and we haven't lost a baby yet."

Francesca smiled.

"I've never traveled by air. Could you tell me what to do?"

"Check your bags here and give me your ticket."

"Here's my ticket, but I have no bags."

The clerk was surprised. She took the ticket, processed it, and handed it back to Francesca.

"Gate number three is that way. The plane will leave in an hour. Have a good trip."

Francesca waited for Jamie, who did not appear. Francesca's heart fell. Her movements became erratic. Feeling her mother's nervousness, Arianna began to cry.

"Shhhh, darling," Francesca whispered.

Then she saw Tony.

Her body felt like jelly. She turned, trying to find a place to hide. Spotting a women's toilet, she ran toward it, but Tony was too fast for her.

"I wouldn't try anything," he warned, motioning to his men to surround her. "Now do as I say, and you won't get hurt."

The look in his eyes caused her to tremble.

"Give me Arianna," he demanded.

"No!" she shrieked.

Several passengers looked around, but Tony's men closed rank around Francesca.

"Don't make a fuss, or you'll get hurt. Give me my baby."

"She's my baby."

"Not any longer. You've forfeited your right to be her mother. I can't trust you, Francesca. You trust a crazy bitch like Jamie. Who knows who you will trust next? The cops? The Feds?"

He took the baby from her. Francesca trembled. Her legs were shaking.

"No!" she screamed.

One of Tony's men pushed her away from the baby. Tony disappeared for several moments. When he returned the baby was gone.

"Where is Arianna?" she asked.

"She's safe. Francesca, I want you to listen to me carefully. You are Arianna's mother, and I don't want you to die. Understand? I respect you for that. But I want you to get on that plane and never come back to New York again. Stay in San Francisco. Go to Italy. Do anything. Here's money. If you need more, contact me. I will pay you to stay away from my child. But if you ever try to contact her, I will have you killed. Do you understand me?"

"What about Arianna? She'll miss me. She loves me."

"Arianna will always be happy. You can count on that."

"But I need her. I love her. Please, Tony, don't do this to me. I thought you loved me."

He looked tortured. His hands trembled, and for a moment he hesitated. Then the familiar strong, stern look returned.

"I love you, Francesca, but I love Arianna more. I need to keep her safe, and I can't watch you all the time. No." He struggled for the right words. "No, this is the best way. I'm sure of it."

"I want to die," she whimpered.

"Go away, Francesca," he said, his voice breaking. *"I never want to see you again."*

PART V

NEW YORK CITY

———————Early Summer———————
1988

ARIANNA

❧ *Chapter 27* ❧

*R*obert Courtney.

Arianna could think of nothing else as she lunched at the Villa Blanca, where owners Enzio Capricio and Sal Marchoni fawned over her. The refrigerator was stocked with her favorite mineral water, and the chef produced pasta with mushrooms flown in specially from Genoa.

Lunch was a respite from the daily discipline aimed at keeping her beautiful. Earlier she had a massage and a personal training session. Daily she catered to her beauty needs: facials, diets, special makeup, and fragrances for scented baths. She loved pampering herself, especially after being self-indulgent. Eating pasta today meant that she must work harder tomorrow.

She relished the Italian custom of eating lunch and strolling afterwards, which grounded her.

Because of the demands of her career, Arianna often felt lost. The toughness necessary to be successful in the music business left her drained. The rock-and-roll world was a jungle dominated by men and drug users. Arianna had to be very strong to compete and succeed.

This world whispered about Arianna. Her songs revealed deep longings, but she was discreet; no one knew about her personal life. It was an Italian custom to keep one's personal life very private.

The media kept trying. Reporters followed her, contacted friends, bribed anyone for news about the Princess of Love.

She was the Princess of Love to fans—but the one man she wanted was avoiding her.

Robert Courtney.

He said she was a spoiled princess and too many men knelt at her feet. He didn't want to be one of them.

Yet he was a fan who loved her songs and had followed her career from punk-rock groups in Lower East Side clubs to her present worldwide fame.

Fame as a Princess of Love—and also as a Mafia princess.

As she signed the lunch check Arianna sipped her espresso and smiled at the waiter. She left the restaurant for her afternoon stroll, a practice common in Italy and continued in many Italian-American communities.

Outside she caused a sensation. Passersby stared at her low-cut silk Giorgio Armani dress, which billowed above the knees. She giggled, wondering how they'd react to her underwear. Underneath the dress she wore a peekaboo black satin corselette. Several cupids were embroidered at cutouts where her nipples were revealed. Another cupid appeared at the bottom of the corselette where her pubic hair was visible.

Because she planned to visit her grandmother, Arianna placed a scarf around her shoulders so that her breasts were covered. Later, she had an all-night rehearsal session, after which she planned to visit Robert. That's why she'd worn sexy undies.

As Arianna walked across the north end of Washington Square Park she spotted the terrace of her father's Lower Fifth Avenue apartment. She hadn't visited her father's apartment for some time, but it was probably still formal and mysterious.

She remembered the last time she had visited the apartment. Two bodyguards were stationed at the door. On a table, one dozen freshly cut roses were arranged beautifully in a red vase. Another dozen in a matching vase were in the living room.

The living room was always in darkness. The blinds were drawn, though the room had a wonderful view of the World Trade Center's twin towers.

She had waited in the living room for her father to return home. There was a photograph of her mother on a handsome white piano, and Arianna entertained herself by picking out tunes she thought her mother might like.

No one had ever given her any information, so Arianna had invented a persona for the deceased woman.

She was kind and gentle. And Arianna missed her.

Now that Arianna was a star, her life was filled with

music, concerts, and crowds. And still she missed her mother.

Her yearning disappeared only when she was at center stage, looking out at the adoring crowd and singing her heart out. She sang of wanting love. All her songs were popular.

She was Arianna—Star.

Afterward, there was always the letdown. Other performers would hole up, drink, and drug out, fearful they wouldn't have the energy to create again. Arianna did not. Instead, her lunches at the Villa Blanca, her strolls through the Village streets, her visits to her grandmother, replenished her energy. These were her roots, and without them she felt empty.

Arianna walked briskly to Houston Street. It was hot, so Arianna decided to change outfits. She stopped at home and took off the Armani dress and the corselette. She chose a soft halter dress and wore nothing underneath.

When Arianna reached her grandmother's apartment building Nanna was leaning on a pillow, looking out the window.

"Hi, Nanna," Arianna called.

"So you came to see your grandmother," she teased.

Upstairs, Arianna hugged the robust woman. Her soft flesh felt like silk sheets tainted by a slight odor of garlic. Antoinette's edict for a long life was to eat a clove of garlic every day. It seemed to work. At seventy-five Antoinette was as vital as ever.

"Nanna, how are you?"

"See what I cooked?"

She pointed to the table where sandwiches fried in olive oil were lying on a large platter.

"Too fattening," Arianna said.

Her grandmother looked indignant. She put her hands on her hips.

"Where did you have lunch?"

"At the Villa Blanca."

Antoinette slapped her forehead with her hand in exasperation.

"Sal cooks better than your grandmother? I knew him when he was a little kid running through the streets. He used to be dirty. I'll bet he's still dirty. You shouldn't eat in his place."

"Nanna, the Villa Blanca is one of the best restaurants in the city."

Antoinette went to the cupboard, took out a box of waxed paper, and carefully wrapped the food.

"I don't know who's going to eat this," she said sadly.

"I'll take it home and eat it later, Nanna."

"Good idea," Antoinette said. "Now tell me what's wrong."

"Nothing."

"Don't lie to me. I've known you since you were a baby. I changed your diapers, listened to your screams, wiped your face, cooked your food."

"What kind of a baby was I?" Arianna asked.

"A good baby," Antoinette said, shaking her head in satisfaction. "Tell me what's wrong."

"It's a man," Arianna said.

"What man?"

"His name is Robert Courtney."

Her grandmother frowned. "He's not Italian."

"No."

"Where is he from?"

"New York."

"Is he Irish?"

"WASP."

"What's WASP?"

"Protestant, English-Scottish."

"You can't marry a Protestant," Nanna said firmly.

"I haven't dated him yet. He doesn't like me."

"Is he crazy? You're beautiful."

"I'm smart, too," Arianna said arrogantly.

"Too smart," Nana countered. "Men don't like smart women."

"You're smart, Nanna."

"But your grandfather never knew it. I raised the family. I kept body and soul together. I worked in the factory. I scrubbed office floors. I took care of him when he was sick. But he never knew it, so he was happy."

"Nanna, I have a problem with men," Arianna said.

"I know," her grandmother agreed, thinking about the effects of stardom.

"It's Papa."

Her grandmother made the Sign Of The Cross.

"Your father is a good man."

"But his business . . . you know how the newspapers play it up."

"A real man wouldn't care about your father. He would only care about you," Antoinette declared.

"I meet lots of men, and they're impressed by my fame. Robert isn't like that."

"Is he rich?"

"Yes."

"Rich people are lucky. If they aren't greedy, they can enjoy their lives."

"He works for abused children."

"What's abused children?"

"Children who are beaten by their parents."

Antoinette crossed herself. How could an adult hurt a child? And how could a man hurt his wife? She thought of poor Francesca. How could George Giotti have treated his wife that way?

"Have you talked to Robert about your father?" Antoinette asked. "He must be a good man if he helps children, so he'll understand that you are not to be judged by your father's life."

"Suppose he's afraid of Papa?" Arianna said.

"There's nothing to be afraid of. My son would never hurt anyone who loves you."

❧ *Chapter 28* ❧

*R*obert Courtney's spacious Park Avenue apartment flowed out in three directions from a wide entrance foyer. Each direction represented a part of his family's existence.

During his lifetime Robert's father, Charles Courtney, had been chairman of the board at Courtney Publications, a collection of twenty-three magazines and trade papers that focused on the fashion industry.

The apartment's left wing held the galleries, a bastion of antique silver, porcelain, brass, jewelry, and whimsies, primarily from the nineteenth century. The study featured an Agra animal rug from India and mirrors that intensified the paisley-patterned walls. A glittery collection of English silver snuffboxes was gathered on a tabletop. On a desk, delicate Nailsea glass pens were fanned out in display, and a Chinese lacquer cabinet housed white Chinese porcelains under a sparkling chandelier.

In the huge living room objects and furniture represented the seventeenth and nineteenth centuries. Several Chippendale armchairs stood alongside a seventeenth-century French beadwork grille. Antique slippers were placed at the foot of each chair, reminding visitors of family ghosts. Next to each chair ledger books served as side tables. On them, Sheffield chambersticks held thin candles.

Robert's late mother, Alma, had shared her husband's passion for the past, but her taste was eclectic. In the dining room were several sideboards containing Chinese, Regency, and Victorian dinnerware. The butler's pantry reflected the same assortment.

A mercurial woman, Alma chose her wardrobe from different couturiers each season, sending her maids into a tizzy. And she often accessorized her ensembles with items from past seasons.

Robert's wing was an iconoclastic mixture of worn-out antiques and sturdy New England furniture. His bedroom was the same room his mother had furnished when he was in college. The walls still held his favorite rock posters. Later he added the modern art bought when he came into two trusts, one from each grandmother.

With his adequate income Robert knew that he didn't have to earn one penny in his lifetime. When his parents died he inherited a controlling interest in Courtney Publications and became a very powerful man.

Robert's heart, however, was not captured by the business, which he turned over to a board of trustees who looked after his interests. The profits climbed, and Robert was one of the least-publicized millionaires in the world. He hired a prestigious public relations firm to keep his name out of the media, for the stigma of being the richest boy at school still haunted him. Robert never knew whether people liked him for his money, for his father's power, or for the intellectuals and movie stars who visited his mother's salon.

His parents led different social lives. His mother kept a penthouse on Lower Fifth Avenue to entertain her artsy friends. She said she needed them to keep a young attitude.

Alma endeavored to help the arts. She completely underwrote the costs of one of the leading ballet companies. She subsidized the careers of two famous painters, financed an opera fashioned after the life of Molly Bloom, James Joyce's creation, and privately published volumes of esoteric poetry and essays about the Victorian age. Because of these interests she was considered a leader in the arts, and she was a patron of the New York Public Library.

Though his parents lived different lives, Robert was sure Charles never looked at another woman. His mother was flighty, eternally curious, and always looking for people who could charm her. Robert never understood how they managed to stay married. Apparently they were devoted to each other. After his father's death his mother died suddenly of a heart attack. And Robert was left very much alone.

Because of his background of money and security, Robert felt he owed something to people who had nothing. When he was freed from parental demands Robert chose to spend his life helping the needy.

He established several foundations, among them the Prince Street Settlement House for Abused Children.

When he became the director of the project he was amazed at how many professional women had abusive histories. Women like Assistant District Attorney Vicki Giotti, who revealed that she was an abused child of a police officer.

This continual exposure to victims led Robert to discipline his own life rigorously. He made precise demands not only upon himself but upon the people he cared about. As a result, though Robert was passionately attracted to Arianna Tucci, he forced himself to resist her.

Early Sunday morning Robert was awakened by his manservant, Yoshita.

"Lady insists on seeing you. Says it's an emergency."

Robert thought about the various emergency situations down at the center. One of the wives, or perhaps one of the children, must be in trouble.

"Who is it?" he asked, his tousled hair framing his slim face, conveying a boyish innocence that belied his thirty-nine years.

"Lady is Ms. Tucci. Says she must see you."

Robert glanced at the clock in the corner of the room. It was seven A.M.

"Tell her to come up," he said. "Would you make a pot of strong coffee?"

He jumped out of bed and went into the shower. His body was lanky but tough. He had been a sickly child. At ten he was told to be cautious for the rest of his life. He worked hard to strengthen his body. He became an amateur boxer at school and enjoyed wrestling, though it was tough on someone as lean as he was. He kept challenging his body to meet physical demands, was careful about nutrition, did not drink or smoke, and worked out daily in the gym located next to his father's former study.

After showering Robert donned a dark blue terry cloth robe and padded about in bare feet. He dried his tousled hair, and its natural curl formed ringlets. When he looked into the mirror his clear blue eyes were troubled. He knew why. He wanted Arianna, but only on his own terms.

Several years earlier his mother had invited him to Le Club because there was a new singer everyone was raving about. After that he returned to listen to Arianna's songs. There was a vulnerable quality in her voice that moved her audience. She strove to be tough, but everyone knew it was her cover.

He watched her meteoric rise in the business, her life haunted by the media coverage of her gangster father. When he finally met her at a fund-raising affair he was falling in love with her.

Looking at his reflection in the bathroom mirror, he steeled himself against the temptation.

Apprehensively, he walked into the living room. Among the antiques Arianna seemed out of place. She was wearing a teal-blue halter dress that barely covered her bosom. As usual, her hair was teased wildly around her lovely porcelain face. Her gorgeous blue eyes were slightly tinted with jade eyeshadow, but the rest of her face looked completely natural.

"What are you doing here, Arianna?" he asked, sitting on the couch.

She was standing in front of the fireplace, tapping her sandaled foot on the marble floor. She moved toward him, then turned around. Robert swore. The halter dress had a tiny strap around her neck that held it in place, but her back was naked down to the end of her spine.

He felt his body grow hard.

"Have you been out all night?" he asked.

"Robert, why are you so hostile?"

Dramatically, she walked over to him. Quickly she opened his robe, taking hold of his hard penis. She stroked it intensely. Then she placed it under her skirt and into her body. She began a soft movement astride him. He felt himself grow larger inside her body. Something stirred in him, and he remembered his resolve to resist her. But the thunderous desire she aroused in him blinded him to everything but the softness of her body and her wanton sensuality.

He closed his eyes and let her make love to him until he erupted inside her. It was his first experience with a sexually aggressive woman. His mind recorded that he disliked the feeling, but his discomfort gave way to the extreme waves of pleasure.

"Arianna." He hid his face in her soft, wild hair.

"Now you make love to me," Arianna whispered.

He pulled at the tiny strap that held her dress. Suddenly the folds of the soft fabric fell, and her large breasts were pulsating against his chest. He buried his face in her heaving bosom. Her body was intensely hot. He could feel the heat from her moist vagina. He kissed one nipple and looked in wonderment when it became hard. He kissed the other breast, held the two breasts together, and kissed them alternately until Arianna moaned with desire.

"Robert, please . . ."

"Yes, my darling," he whispered hoarsely.

Gently, he spread his robe upon his father's favorite couch and placed her upon it. She put her mouth on his organ. He leaned back to enjoy it, then said, "No, not that way. I want to be inside you." She lay back on the couch, and he placed his beating organ inside her hot vagina. She began a sucking motion with her vaginal lips that sent him wild. He felt as if he were lost inside of her and that she would never let him go. He begged for more as she held his penis fast, rubbing against him in the most incredible motion that sent electrifying waves throughout his body, beginning at the top of his head, charging the genital area, and moving down to his toes. His entire body was consumed by waves of sexual energy. He lost control and became savage. He thrust into her violently. Her legs wound about his waist as he lifted her from the couch. She screamed a loud, primitive sound that awakened the room's ghosts. He felt surrounded by his past, his present, and his future. When she screamed again he remembered the mating sounds of tigers he had heard when he was on an African safari.

He wanted to give her everything he could from the depth of his soul, for he knew he had met his nemesis. Other women faded in his memory. Arianna was different. He had read about her, dreamt about her, fantasized about her. Now she was here.

"Love me," she whispered.

With every ounce of his energy he thrust into her again and again. Finally he lost control and emptied himself into her pulsating body.

* * *

When she awoke from a deep sleep Robert was still beside her. Arianna watched him. His face was lean, his lips were taut, yet as he slept a blissful look softened his features. It was an interesting contrast to his normal appearance. Awake, he had the craggy look of a hunter, a fisherman, or a pioneer, conveying strength.

Satiated, she moaned. She had set out to seduce the elusive Robert and accomplished her mission. She rose from the couch, but Robert's arm shot out and pinned her down.

"Arianna," he asked, "what do you want?"

She kissed him lightly on the tip of his elegant nose and laughed.

"More of the same, Robert, dear," she teased.

"If you only want sex, go somewhere else," he said angrily.

He pushed her away so hard that she fell to the floor. He rose and put on his robe quickly, as if to protect his body from her sensuousness.

"That's the first time I've been pushed out of bed," she laughed.

She began dressing, but the string of the halter dress was broken.

"Do you have something I can wear?"

He turned to her, his face angry.

"Arianna, stop acting like a silly bimbo. You're a gorgeous woman. You're talented. And you have a heart."

"Oh, do I?"

"You couldn't write those wonderful songs if you didn't feel deeply about things. Look at me." He held her tightly and insisted that she look into his face. "I want you, Arianna. Can you handle that?"

She wanted to say yes, Robert, I want you, too, but a familiar feeling consumed her. A faint memory—a deep, warm love—and then nothing. Fear gripped her. She was afraid that if she loved him, he would disappear.

"Let's keep it cool," she said.

"Arianna, that's not good enough. If that's what you want, I'm out."

"Oh, it's love?" she said softly.

"Yes, it's love," he whispered.

She panicked, enveloped by a sense of aloneness. She couldn't let him go. She wanted him. But did he love her, or did he love Arianna, the star she had created?

"Robert, is it me you want? Or is it Arianna?"

"You're one person."

"No, Arianna is strong and sure and talented. I'm not that way. I'm Tough Tony Tucci's daughter. I'm an Italian girl. I'm secretive and scared and . . ."

"You're like everyone else, darling," he said.

"Am I?" she asked in a tiny voice.

"Try to trust me, Arianna. Can you do that?" he asked gently.

"It's hard for me to trust anyone."

"We have something very special. Let's promise each other that we won't let anything change that."

Tears fell on her soft cheeks. "Robert, you do care," she whispered.

"Hush, darling," he whispered. "Let's not talk anymore."

Chapter 29

*T*he media hasn't let up for a minute, Stu. I'm out of here," Arianna said angrily into the phone. "I'm packing my bag and going someplace far away."

"You can't do that, babe. We have the concert hall booked. It's showtime, Arianna. The hell with the media."

"They've called every half hour since they found Giotti in the church. What am I? Sixty Mafia Minutes?" she complained.

"Whenever something happens involving your father they hassle you. You should know that by now."

"I'm not going to be intimidated by those hacks."

"That's my girl. Look, I have a space in Brooklyn where no one can find us. We can rehearse while your father's mess gets straightened out. By showtime, we'll be ready."

"Good thinking. But how can I leave the town

house? They're swarming around outside, and I don't have a back entrance."

"Don't worry, I'll send a limo and bodyguards pronto. Pack a few things. We're going into isolation."

"Sounds good to me."

"You're the star," Stu said. "See you."

As Arianna packed the phone rang. Thinking it might be Robert, she answered it.

"Your father has gone into hiding," Mary Adams said. "Does this mean that he's responsible for the murder of George Giotti?"

Arianna slammed down the phone. There had been no word from her father since the Giotti murder hit the headlines. She was waiting for someone to contact her in person, knowing her father was too careful to use the phone. Meanwhile, she tried not to think about the Giotti murder.

When Arianna had become a star, she put up a survival wall between her life and her father's.

She was like him. She made her own rules and lived her life the way she wanted to and answered to no one.

But now there was Robert. She hoped the headlines wouldn't sway his love. Robert had been out of town when the Giotti body was discovered, and she hadn't been able to reach him though his secretary said he was back.

"The limo is here," her housekeeper, Martha, announced.

"Please remember to visit Nanna. If the media bothers her, phone me. If anyone comes from my father, you know what to do."

"Be careful," Martha said.

Arianna picked up the bags, put on large dark glasses, and opened the door. Immediately the bodyguards escorted her into the waiting limo. Arianna told the driver to stop at the Prince Street Settlement House. She must tell Robert that she would be incommunicado.

At the settlement house the receptionist recognized her.

"Arianna," she said breathlessly.

"I must see Robert Courtney."

"He's in conference in his office."

Arianna ran quickly up the stairs. Whe she reached Robert's office she opened the door with a bright smile of welcome on her face.

But her smile faded quickly. Arianna blinked her eyes in disbelief. Seated next to Robert, with her head on his shoulder, was Vicki Giotti.

Before Robert could say a word, Arianna fled.

Vicki had appeared in Robert's office without an appointment, knowing he was always available to volunteers. They had become friends when Vicki worked on a fund-raising campaign for the Abused Children Project, despite her rigorous schedule at the district attorney's office. During the campaign Vicki told Robert about her experiences as an abused child.

When he heard about George Giotti's death, Robert's experience told him that Vicki might be ambivalent, feeling both relief and guilt. He heard she'd been released from the hospital a few days earlier, so he wasn't surprised to see her at his office. When she took off her sunglasses her eyes were red and swollen.

"I heard the news on my way back from the airport," he said, putting an arm around her to comfort her.

"Robert, I don't understand it. He was a terrible father. I hated him. He mistreated me. Why have I spent the night crying for him?"

"Because he was your father," Robert said quietly. "And you loved him."

She began sobbing again. When she stopped, he wiped her eyes dry.

"Do the police know who killed him?" Robert asked.

"They found a gun behind the altar registered to Tony Tucci."

Robert froze. He thought of Arianna and the pain this would cause her.

"Are they sure it's Tucci's gun?"

"His lawyers say the gun was stolen years ago. We don't think Tucci actually pulled the trigger, but the gun gives us the opportunity to question him. But Tucci has disappeared."

"You're going to let your colleagues handle this, aren't you?"

Her beautiful eyes were still.

"No, Robert. I'm taking a leave of absence. I have to find my father's killer."

"Are you sure you want to go through this? If you get involved in finding your father's killer, all the bad feelings will return. Do you want that?"

Robert knew Vicki's feelings were unresolved because he had tried to get her to consult a therapist. The center had several therapists who specialized in the strange bonding that occurred between abused children and their oppressors. Vicki refused, saying that she didn't believe in therapy or in irrational emotions. That's why Robert tried to be an informal counselor to Vicki, as he was to many of the center's clients.

"Finding my father's murderer will free me," Vicki insisted.

"And if you don't find your father's murderer?"

"I'll have to live with this awful guilt," she said sadly.

She bit her lips nervously, then spoke in a trembling voice.

"There's something I want you to know. I'm going to have a baby."

"Will this baby have a father?" Robert asked, knowing that Vicki had hired Paul Johnson.

"Paul wants to continue seeing me."

"Why not, Vicki?"

"I'm afraid that any man I choose won't be a good father. I couldn't survive that."

"What about Vito Marchese?"

"Vito is a good guy, but I can't trust any man. Can you understand that?"

"Yes," he said. "Vicki, is there anything I can do?"

"Be a good friend. That's what I need. I don't have anyone to talk to. I can't talk to my aunts. They won't hear a word against my father."

"I'll be here," he promised.

"Thanks," Vicki said gratefully, putting her head on his shoulder.

As he tightened his arms around her Robert's eyes grew misty. This was the kind of reward that business did not bring. Working with people made him feel alive in a very special way. That's why he loved the center.

Behind him he heard a door open. He twisted his head to see who was there.

From the doorway Arianna stared at him with disbelief in her eyes. Before he could call out to her she was gone.

Chapter 30

*T*he six members of Arianna's band arrived late at the Brooklyn studio. The lead guitarist stepped out of a white stretch limo wrapped in a long white coat and accompanied by a tall redhead named Lauren. His name was Kirk, and he liked to order his men about.

"Hey, buddy, get your act together," he called to Sandy, the keyboardist.

"We've learned to hate him," Sandy deadpanned as he took his place in the studio.

His bandmates, Tony, the bassist and Harry, the drummer, joined him to sniff coke. Watching them, Arianna was livid.

"Are you going to be ready soon?" she shouted, holding earphones tightly to her ears.

Jo Jo went to her side.

"You know how long it takes them to get started.

Once they get going it's going to be a great session."

"I'm running out of energy," she said angrily.

Jo Jo signaled Stu to expect trouble. Arianna was in a tizzy. Jo Jo learned from the limo driver that she had made an unscheduled stop at the Prince Street Settlement House. He guessed something had happened between Robert and Arianna. That's why she was acting weird. Normally Arianna had positive energy at rehearsals. Today she was in a real fury. The stuff about her father probably added to her mood, though Jo Jo knew Arianna was used to that kind of flack.

"Come on, mates," Jo Jo said to the band, "how about it?"

They ignored Jo Jo. Well, he knew how to deal with that.

"Do you want to be docked for the extra time?" he asked.

Grumbling, the group tuned up. Soon they were rocking and Arianna was singing. As Stu listened he felt an incredible excitement grow with each take. When the first break was called Jo Jo whispered in Stu's ear, and he turned pale.

"Where?" Stu asked.

"The entrance."

Arianna, exhausted, was wiping her face with a towel.

"There's someone to see you, Arianna," Stu said.

"I thought no one knew about this place," she said.

"So did I. It's one of your father's men."

"Where is he?"

"At the door."

Arianna walked down the corridor toward the door of the converted warehouse. When she saw Bustero Da Costa she smiled.

"Uncle Bustero."

She kissed him on both cheeks. The short, squat man grinned. His beak nose was red from drinking too much wine.

"Your father sent me. He's taking a trip until this blows over," Bustero explained.

"They say he murdered George Giotti."

"Don't worry about that. He has an alibi."

"I hope it's reliable."

"It is. I came to give you a message. Your father wants you to cancel this concert. Arianna, he's not sure who's behind this attempt to frame him for Giotti's murder. Some of the new men can't be trusted to follow the rules. You might be in danger."

"Tell my father to stay out of my life," she said angrily.

"He's worried about your safety, Arianna."

She shrugged her shoulders. "He's always worried about my safety. Don't worry, I can take care of myself."

Backstage was pandemonium. Arianna was in her dressing room alone. Her staff was outside, giving her the private time she required. Stu was pacing while Jo Jo tried to calm him down. Stu noticed several construction crews near the stage door and decided they were undercover cops waiting for Tucci to show up at Arianna's concert. Tucci always attended Arianna's concerts, watching her performance from a box. Tonight Stu prayed that Tucci wouldn't attend.

A security man told Stu someone wanted to see Arianna before the concert.

"Who is it?" Stu asked.

"Robert Courtney."

"This guy gets to her," Jo Jo advised.

"Keep him away," Stu said to the guard.

The man nodded. Robert Courtney was escorted out of the theater and told to stay away.

It was showtime. Onstage, dressed in a scanty costume with a towering headdress of dyed feathers, Arianna was mesmerizing.

The lights go out, and it's you and me and all the kinds of things we like to do. Give me lessons, darling. Hold me close and tell me how to love you. Tell me, baby. Tell me. I need to know.

The audience screamed the chorus, "Yes, I need to know." She was singing passionately. The result was an exciting rock-and-roll performance, one that combined the rebellious fury of adolescence with the calm arrogance of knowing all the answers.

I'm scared of being without you. You love me. Now that you do, what will I be? Will I be happy? Will I be lonely?

Clouds of red smoke billowed from the stage as Arianna danced like a female satyr. The band was in darkness except for the lights glinting off their instruments as they accompanied Arianna's frenzied dance of love. The audience screeched their adoration of Arianna. With exaggerated passion she blew kisses as her eyes strayed over the crowd. She couldn't see them in the darkness, but she could feel the love they sent in great waves of energy. She shuddered with the strange exhilaration that always possessed her when she performed. It was different from recording songs; it was different from writing songs. A concert was alive, and there was no feeling in the world like it.

On stage Arianna was on top of the world, above pain, above fear, surrounded by adoring love. Here nothing could harm her.

She was all spirit, all genius, all goddess.

She was Arianna. Star.

Suddenly a spark from the audience caught her eye. Behind her Kirk called, "Arianna, watch out!" She turned toward him, but her smile froze. Kirk stood strangely still. The front of his silk shirt burst open with a rush of blood. He fell to his knees. Jo Jo ran from the wings, grabbed Arianna, and shielded her from the audience. He pulled her offstage as Sandy slammed gracefully against his drums. Thinking this was part of the performance, the audience screamed. Then Sandy's back arched. He threw up his arms and slid forward, pitching toward the crowd. His blood ran freely, spraying the front row of the audience. When the people saw it was real blood they panicked.

Backstage Arianna was trembling.

"Someone tried to kill you," Jo Jo whispered.

"Let's get out of here."

Her body shook violently as Jo Jo covered her with his coat. He called out to Stu.

"Get the limo. We have to leave before the cops arrive."

Jo Jo escorted Arianna to the stage door, where the fans and media waited who were not aware of what had happened inside the concert hall. Among them was Robert Courtney.

When Arianna saw him she screamed, "Robert, help me!"

Sensing her terror, he pushed his way through the crowd swiftly. Against Jo Jo's objections he picked her up and carried her into the waiting limo.

🍂 Chapter 31 🍂

*A*rianna paced. For four days she hadn't eaten, slept, or taken a shower. She screamed, or sat silent with her arms folded, or wept like a baby. Through each phase Robert spoke to her gently. When the periods between the hysterical fits lengthened Robert was able to get her to eat. Exhausted, she fell asleep for thirty-six hours. When she awoke Robert held her close.

"Feel like talking?" he asked.

She nodded.

"I've never been afraid of anything. I was spoiled. My father gave me every material thing I ever wanted. I told myself I could have anything because I was Tony Tucci's daughter. But I never had friends. My father wouldn't even let me play with my cousins. He said I was better than other children. I was the princess in the tower. But I was lonely.

"When I grew up I wanted to be part of a family. That's why I love singing with the band. I created Arianna, the Princess of Love. I thought I was happy. But it was all an act. The act worked until I fell in love with you. When I saw you with Vicki Giotti . . ."

"Vicki comes to me for advice. I try to help her. Her father was an abusive parent."

"She must be happy that her father is dead."

"It's not that simple. Abused children hate their tormentors, but they love them, too."

"That's how I feel about my father. I thought I was the only one who was mixed up."

"Arianna, love isn't perfect or simple."

"We always love the wrong people, Robert. That's what my songs are about."

He kissed her passionately.

"Darling, we're right for each other. Remember, it's uncomfortable to trust someone. When you saw me with Vicki you could have asked me about her. You're always surrounded by lots of men, aren't you?" She nodded her head in agreement. "I'm going to have to deal with that. And you're going to have to deal with the fact that I have other relationships that require my attention and love. But you're the woman I love and want to live with."

"I'll try, Robert," she whispered.

Several weeks passed before Arianna agreed to talk to the police. Afterward the police told Robert that they believed the attempted shooting was connected to a struggle for power within the Mafia.

The funeral for the dead band members was a media event, and Arianna's absence was duly noted. The networks broadcast a special on her career featuring dated newspaper photos of the body of Don Allegro after he was shot by Policeman George Giotti at Arianna's baptism. The media alluded to this earlier shooting as the reason that Tucci killed Giotti.

Arianna and Robert watched the television coverage.

"It doesn't make sense," Arianna protested. "If my father wanted to murder George Giotti, why did he wait all these years?"

Suddenly a faded photograph appeared on the screen as the television reporter said, "This is Tony Tucci's wife, rumored to have disappeared mysteriously years ago. There is talk that she may have been killed."

"My mother died in childbirth," Arianna said.

"There must be hospital records."

She shook her head. "I was delivered by a midwife at home. My father explained the whole thing to me."

"But there has to be a death certificate."

Abruptly, she switched off the set. Robert looked thoughtful. This was something he would look into.

After the funeral of Arianna's band members she knew it was time to go back to her life, but she didn't want to return to the town house. The media was still camped outside.

"Live with me, Arianna," Robert said. "Let's get married."

"Not now," she said somberly.

"Why not?"

"Let's wait until this mess blows over."

"Okay. But you have to get back to work."

"I don't feel like singing," she said.

"It'll be good for you to perform. You're happy when you're working. I have an idea. We're having a party for the project. Why don't you perform for the children?"

"I'm scared, Robert," she said.

"Don't worry, darling. You'll be a sensation," Robert promised.

Vicki Giotti was asking her street sources about Tucci's whereabouts. When word got back to Vito he phoned Vicki to warn her to stay out of the Tucci investigation.

"The boss is going to be very angry if he hears about it, honey."

"Don't call me honey," she said. "And I don't care what he thinks."

"You don't mean that. Besides, Tucci didn't pull the trigger. His lawyers say he has an airtight alibi."

"Why did he go into hiding?"

"He's being cautious. He's waiting for his lawyers to discredit the gun evidence." Vito paused, then added, "We're not telling the media about this, Vicki."

When she hung up Vicki realized that since she wasn't working on the case she had no obligation to be discreet. If she could get Tucci angry enough, he might blow his cover. She dialed Mary Adams.

"I owe you one," Adams said when she heard Vicki's news. "Do you know that Arianna and Robert Courtney are having a mad affair? Aren't you a friend of his?"

"I was," Vicki answered.

*   *   *

"Give it up, Vicki," Robert insisted.

"How can you be involved with Arianna Tucci? I know you like to help people who are in trouble, but Arianna is a gangster's daughter. He's in the Mafia."

"Arianna is not involved in her father's business."

"But she's part of the family. Everything he touches turns bloody. You've been a good friend, and I'm simply trying to return the favor."

"I love Arianna," he said.

"Robert, you aren't serious."

"Yes, I am. I want Arianna, and she wants me."

"I can't believe it," she said. "You've fallen for a bimbo."

"Vicki," Robert said sternly, "I can't allow you to insult Arianna in my presence. We're going to be married."

She stared at him in disbelief.

"This will ruin your life," she said ominously.

"Love never ruins our lives. It's hate that ruins lives. If you don't give up your hate for the Tuccis, your baby is going to be born into an unhappy world."

"Like I was?" she taunted. "A world of hate and fear and beatings and no one to take care of me. No, that won't happen to my baby because she won't have any men in her life."

"You know that it's not only men who abuse children."

"Are you saying that I could do that to my baby?" Vicki said furiously.

"If you don't heal the terrible scars from your childhood, sooner or later your baby will become part of your hell."

She stared at him angrily. Then she walked out of his office.

She had tried to talk sense into Robert, but there was no reaching him. Arianna had her claws into Robert, and he was beyond reason. That's what happened when people fell in love.

Arianna sang two songs, watching the faces of the children light up. They were a varied lot. Some were poor, some well-dressed, but all had a ravaged look on their faces. Some clung to a parent who had abused them. Some sat separately, moving away whenever a parent tried to touch them.

"Sing 'Heartsick,' " one child requested.

Arianna looked at Robert. They had decided that she wouldn't sing rock-and-roll tunes because her audience was young. But he nodded, and she sang the salty tune that had established her reputation.

"I want you," she sang, *"and I want your love."*

There were loud noises from the first floor of the settlement house. Arianna heard the insistent sounds of the media. Quickly, she glanced at Robert. He walked over to her.

"Don't worry, Arianna. I'll keep those bastards out of here."

When he reached the first floor he saw the reporters waiting outside the settlement house entrance. Robert walked outside to speak to them.

"You're not permitted inside, so why don't you leave?" he suggested.

There was a howl from the TV crews. "Come on, we're just doing our job," one man said.

"Is it true that you're involved with Arianna Tucci?" Mary Adams asked on camera.

"I am," he said.

Another reporter shoved a mike in Robert's face.

"What is your relationship?" he asked.

"We're going to be married."

"Does the fact that your fiancée's father is suspected of murdering a cop affect your plans?" Mary Adams asked vehemently.

"My fiancée's father is under investigation, and I don't want to comment."

"Will Tough Tony come to the wedding?" Adams continued.

"I don't know," Robert answered.

The woman sat in the motel room on Manhattan's West Side watching the television coverage. A smile appeared on her somber face when she heard Robert Courtney's remark. She picked up the phone and dialed. When a man's voice answered she spoke quickly.

"Our daughter is getting married, Tony. It's on television."

"Yes, I saw it."

"You must give yourself up."

"My lawyers say they need more time," he answered.

"Arianna is going to be married. We must clear up this mess. I want her to be happy."

"Are you sure you're not thinking of Victoria Regina?" he demanded.

Her heart beat rapidly. Even after all these years, when he spoke, her first instinct was to obey. If she did, then the many years spent forging herself into a different woman would be wasted.

She breathed deeply, then spoke.

"I'm thinking of both my daughters, Tony," she said adamantly. "You must come out of hiding, or I'll go to the media," she threatened.

"Francesca—"

But the phone went dead.

PART VI

NEW YORK CITY

1954

FRANCESCA

❧ Chapter 32 ❧

Sweat saturated Francesca's body. Her legs trembled as she ran into the airport ladies' room. She felt cold and clammy and, standing unsteadily at a sink, gave in to nausea. She splashed cold water on her face. When she looked into the mirror her ghostly reflection frightened her. She hyperventilated, feeling as though the oxygen in her lungs was stifled. She tried to breathe deeply, but her chest felt like a knot of steel. Panicked, she gasped, her balance unsteady.

"Are you all right?" The crisp voice broke into Francesca's horror. Standing at the next sink was a middle-aged woman.

"I . . . I . . ."

"Try to relax," the woman said softly.

Francesca's head throbbed as the stranger held out her hand. Francesca grasped it—a lifeline to sanity.

"When I feel ill I use these." The woman held rosary beads in her other hand.

Memories deluged Francesca's consciousness. Her white rosary beads on her first Holy Communion day. She wore a wonderful dress with two organdy skirts and a ruffled jacket, and she felt like a princess. Her mother said it was the only day, aside from marriage, when a girl could feel a special way.

"What way?" young Francesca asked.

"Happy," Matilda answered.

Afterward Francesca tried to hold on to the feeling, but it was fleeting. It returned when she gave birth to Victoria Regina, and again at Arianna's birth.

The thought of her loved ones caused Francesca anguish. Arianna and Victoria Regina were a part of her. And now they were to be separated forever.

And it was her fault.

"I deserve to die," Francesca muttered.

Gently, the woman squeezed Francesca's hand.

"May I help?"

Francesca looked at the slim, attractive woman. Her outfit was tailored and expensive, her hair short and stylish.

"Have you been ill?" the woman asked.

"Life hasn't treated me well."

"Would you like to talk?"

Hesitantly, Francesca looked into the woman's compassionate eyes.

"You're wondering whether you can trust me. Perhaps I should tell you that I'm about to become a nun," the woman said.

Francesca watched the woman's hand moving from one prayer bead to another. Young Francesca had been taught to pray. Always trust God, the sisters said. Francesca liked church because it made her feel peaceful. After her first marriage she stopped attending mass. When she remarried she transferred her faith to her new husband. And Tony failed her, as God had.

"You may think you're forsaken, but you're not," the woman said softly. "My name is Teresa Drocci. You're Italian, aren't you?"

"Yes."

"From Italy?"

"My parents were born there, but they've lived in New York for many years."

"Mine are from Florence. There are many beautiful frescoes there. You remind me of a *Madonna and Child*." She paused. "What's your name?"

"Francesca Cella."

"That's a lovely name."

"Where's your convent?"

"Peekskill. Have you been there?"

Suddenly Francesca burst into harsh tears.

"I've lost my babies," she cried.

"Let's go into the restaurant," Teresa suggested. "We'll have something to eat. You'll feel better."

In the airport restaurant Teresa sipped coffee as Francesca tried to eat. Watching her, Teresa sensed the young woman was in real trouble.

"Let me tell you about myself," Teresa said. "I'm a concert pianist. I've played in concert halls throughout the world. Then I had an accident. The doctors said I might lose my hands. God spared them, so I vowed to serve Him. Since then I've been very happy."

"How?" Francesca whispered.

"God will help you, too." She touched Francesca's trembling hands. "Now tell me what's troubling you."

Francesca told Teresa about Tony's abduction of Arianna.

"Go to court. The law is always on the mother's side."

"You can't win against the Mafia," Francesca said hopelessly.

"Why not?"

"There are things I can't tell you. Anyhow, it's all my fault. I've sinned too many times, and God is punishing me. I abandoned my Victoria Regina." Her voice broke as tears fell from her lovely eyes. "I fell in love with Tony and left my baby girl. I deserve to be punished."

"You're too hard on yourself. God forgives our sins, if we ask Him." Teresa gave Francesca the rosary beads. "Hold them. They'll make you feel better."

"I can't win," Francesca repeated morosely. "Men have all the power. That's what Jamie says, and she's right."

"Jamie is wrong. People have power only if we give it to them. Remember, our Lord said the meek will inherit the earth."

"Then I'll be a millionaire," Francesca said sarcastically.

Teresa looked worried. "Do you have somewhere to go?"

"I was going to California. But now—"

"Come to the convent with me. I know God will help you."

"No one can help me."

"Nothing is hopeless in God's eyes. We'll pray for your daughters."

"What good will prayers do? They need me. How can my babies grow up without a mother?"

"Francesca, you have to fight for what you want in life."

"I don't have the strength."

"Trust me. God has a plan for you, I can promise you that. It's not an accident that we met."

"No one can change things," Francesca insisted.

"Someone can."

"Who?" Francesca asked.

"You," Teresa answered.

Even in the heat of summer birds sang as they flew through the lush trees shading the gardens of the Convent of the Sacred Heart. Blue hydrangeas cuddled behind white roses along one side of the spacious lawn. Enormous trees stretched their branches over the manicured grass. At the far end was a border of lilies, pale malvas, and blue cornflowers. Tall, dark hedges protected the terrace, and picket fences took up where the hedges left off. The fences held an enchanting rose-wreathed trellis.

Francesca worked steadily next to the shingled gardener's hut, filling window boxes with hollyhocks, snapdragons, daisies, and blue salvia. The boxes were to be installed at the window of each bedroom so that the nuns could see flowers the first thing each morning.

Francesca's outfit was not cool. Her shirt had long sleeves and a high collar. Her wide skirt was down to her ankles. Her shoes were low-heeled but too stiff for gardening. She rolled up her sleeves and dug her fingers into the moist earth.

She was a novice at country living, and the dark earth was one of the first things that attracted her. She also loved the sense of order.

At the Convent of the Sacred Heart everything was planned. Each period of the day was scheduled. The sisters were summoned by a series of bells. They hurried to chapel or class with prayers on their lips. They were a part of one another.

After she took her vows Sister Teresa spoke of being part of the body of Christ along with the other nuns.

Sister Teresa had been brought up in an upper-crust, bilingual home. Rich and socially accepted around the world, she gave it all up for God. She explained that her life had to count for something.

Sister Teresa was wonderful to Francesca and arranged for a job in the convent's kitchen for a small salary plus room and board.

At first Francesca cried each night for her babies. But things changed. She didn't know whether it was the trees, the flowers, the brook, or the chapel, but one morning she felt a sense of peace.

Sister Teresa said it was her renewed faith.

After several months Francesca believed Sister Teresa because there was no other explanation for the degree of happiness she experienced. She sang while she worked in the kitchen. She smiled at everyone. When she thought about Arianna and Victoria Regina, she prayed for them with hope.

But she yearned to know what was happening to them. Sister Teresa suggested that she write to her mother. Francesca knew Matilda could not keep secrets. Then she thought of someone who could.

She wrote to Antoinette Tucci. A month later she received a letter with the news that both Arianna and Vicki were fine. The ritual continued. Month after month she received treasured notes about her children.

One day Mother Mary called Francesca into the office. The pink-cheeked nun was in charge of the convent.

"Francesca, have you been happy here?"

"Yes, I have."

"I know that you love the gardens. Would you like to care for them?"

"I don't know anything about flowers."

"The gardener at St. Thomas Monastery will teach you. Would you like that?"

"Yes, Mother," Francesca said.

She worked hard and didn't mind that her fingernails were always dirty, no matter how much soap and water she scrubbed them with.

Working in the garden gave Francesca a sense of purpose. After several years the garden became a source of great pride, and people flocked to see it.

As time passed Antoinette sent photographs of Arianna. It was difficult for her to get photographs of Victoria Regina, but she managed to obtain one occasionally. Francesca placed the photographs near her bed. Each night she had conversations with her daughters.

One day Francesca opened one of Antoinette's letters and found a newspaper clipping about Jamie

Jamison, who had been found dead in her apartment. The police suspected homicide.

Francesca trembled. Was Jamie's death connected to Tony? Her past returned to haunt her. Chaos touched the lives of everyone she loved. Jamie—her brave, courageous friend—was dead.

That night Francesca wept for Jamie. When she worked in the gardens the next morning she thanked God for giving her refuge. She could never go back to her other life.

It was too dangerous.

❧ Chapter 33 ❧

The years flew by quickly, and Antoinette steadfastly sent Francesca news and photographs. As each daughter graduated from high school Antoinette mailed their yearbooks. Arianna was a beauty, and Victoria Regina had a certain gracefulness.

Francesca wrote Antoinette asking if the girls were friendly. Antoinette answered that they lived in two different worlds.

During the late sixties Francesca prayed that Arianna and Victoria Regina were not part of the drug culture. Though she lived far from the world's turmoil, students visited her garden. From them she learned about nudity, peace marches, and flower children.

A few years later students talked about feminism, which reminded Francesca of Jamie. Jamie had been a pioneer, viewing the world as sexist before it was fashionable. Francesca knew that Jamie would be happy about the feminist movement.

Francesca felt proud when Antoinette wrote that Victoria Regina was attending law school. The older woman worried about Arianna, who left school to sing rock-and-roll.

As Arianna's career blossomed Francesca visited the Peekskill library to read newspapers and magazines. When Victoria Regina was appointed to the District Attorney's office her name was in the newspapers, too.

Francesca was proud of her daughters, who were a different breed of women. They were strong despite the unhappiness their childhood had brought them.

One day, in the library, Francesca picked up a newspaper and read the words that would destroy her peaceful and calm existence:

Retired policeman George Giotti was found shot to death in St. Anthony's Church. The police suspect a Mafia hit. Tough Tony Tucci's gun was found on the premises. Tucci has gone into hiding.

Trembling, Francesca read the story that suggested the murder was a vendetta connected to the Don Allegro assassination by policeman Giotti. This incident occurred at St. Anthony's when Tucci's daughter, the rock-and-roll star Arianna Tucci, was baptized.

Oh, God, Francesca thought, it's going to start all over again.

Through the years Francesca had felt her daughters were safe because no one in the neighborhood would reveal information. After all, Tony was a mafioso.

But if the media exploited the Giotti–Tucci affair, someone might come forward. And if reporters dug up the truth, her daughters might never recover from the shock.

That night Francesca slipped out of the convent, quietly lingering in the beautiful gardens.

The time for peace was over. She must return.

Her daughters needed her.

PART VII

NEW YORK CITY

———————Late Summer———————
1988

❧ *Chapter 34* ❧

*W*hat proof do you have?"

Vicki asked questions like an attorney, but Mother Teresa responded with compassion.

"Francesca had a recurring dream," the nun explained. "In it she walked in the gardens along the path where the flowers gather in a border around the statue of Jesus. Behind this statue is a fountain. Each morning the birds flock there. Francesca watched the mother birds chirping lovely songs to their young."

Mother Teresa's eyes grew teary as she related the dream to Arianna and Vicki.

"In Francesca's dream she was the mother bird and you were the baby birds. She wanted to care for you until you were grown and could be on your own."

"That's not much proof," Vicki scoffed.

But Arianna's eyes filled with tears. Her cheeks

reddened as the moisture carved a thin line through her makeup.

"What a lovely story." Arianna hummed. " 'Mother Bird Fly to Me.' That's a great tune."

Warmly, Mother Teresa smiled at Arianna. Then she spoke directly to Vicki.

"I do have hard evidence, Victoria Regina," the nun said.

Vicki grew pale as her eyes darted furtively from Arianna to the nun. Her body was bent forward in a defensive position. She kneaded her fingers as she spoke.

"No one has ever called me that," she whispered.

"That's your true name. It's on your birth certificate."

Trapped, Vicki looked down and studied a nearby patch of grass. Finally she looked up at the nun.

"Yes, that's my name, but I don't use it. Still," she continued as if she were arguing a court case, "an old neighbor might know about my real name. Perhaps Francesca found out . . ."

"I know it's chic to suspect people nowadays," Mother Teresa interrupted. "It was different when I was young. We had faith in people. We had to have proof that someone was evil."

"I appreciate that, Mother," Vicki said harshly as she paced.

Arianna watched her with an amused look.

"What are you smirking at?" Vicki demanded.

"It's good to see you stew," Arianna countered. "You're always winning cases. You pretend that you never make mistakes. It's nice to see that the very cool Vicki Giotti is human."

"You're a birdbrain," Vicki said viciously. "If you were in my profession, you'd wake up from your fantasy world. I know mothers who kill babies. I know sons and daughters who cheat old parents out of money. I know children who kill other children over drugs. I know reality."

"We all do," Arianna said seriously. Her elegant fingernails caught the sunlight as she pointed to Vicki. "The trouble with you legal types is that you assume you know right from wrong."

"That's right."

"All you know is what works in court and what doesn't. You don't know about people. You don't care that my father has good qualities."

"Does he?" Vicki laughed. "He owns the gun that killed my father. I'm going to get him on that little item."

Arianna walked toward Vicki in a threatening manner.

"That gun was stolen years ago. You're jumping to conclusions because he's Tony Tucci. If he were John Smith, you'd look for real evidence. Anything that screams Mafia makes lawyers crave fame and glory."

"They're animals," Vicki said with rage.

"They're people. They have families who will be hurt. Don't you ever think of that?"

They were an interesting duo. Mother Teresa thought Arianna was better suited for the role of attorney. She exhibited a passion for the truth. Vicki seemed more like a preacher.

"You won't ever do anything wrong, will you, Ms. Giotti?" Arianna baited.

Mother Teresa's shoulders tensed as she watched.

She knew that Francesca hoped her daughters might comfort each other when they learned the truth.

"Your mother wants you to be friends," the nun said.

Both wore a look of denial and belief that reflected their ambivalence.

"I don't believe in fairy tales," Vicki said.

"I do," Arianna retorted. "Tell me more about Francesca."

"See that bush of white roses?" Mother Teresa pointed to a rosebush growing among the roses of darker hues. "That's what Francesca's like. She's very pure. She believes that love must be given without conditions. That's why she didn't know how to fight for you."

"Why couldn't she?" Vicki asked earnestly.

"I don't want to insult your father, Vicki, but Francesca said he was very brutal."

"He was a brutal man," Vicki admitted.

Arianna looked at Vicki with interest.

"Was he a bad father?" she asked.

"He was an alcoholic. When he drank he couldn't control his temper," Vicki said, and she patted her stomach nervously.

"Was he brutal to you?" Mother Teresa asked, noticing her gesture.

"Sometimes," Vicki admitted. She turned to Arianna. "When I told Robert that I was an abused child he explained why I both loved and hated my father."

"I feel the same way about my father," Arianna said.

"I didn't know that."

They smiled at each other for the first time.

"I guess we're human," Arianna said. Then she turned to the nun. "Where is Francesca? Even if she isn't my mother, I'd like to meet her."

"She's your mother," Mother Teresa said.

She took two sheets of paper from an envelope and handed one to each woman. They studied their birth certificates in disbelief.

"My father told me my mother's name was Matilda," Vicki murmured.

"That's your grandmother's name," Mother Teresa explained.

"I remember a woman . . . Matilda . . . she came to the park. . . ."

Mother Teresa nodded.

"Your father refused to allow your mother to see you, so Matilda checked on you."

"I remember my mother," Vicki murmured.

"You were two when she was separated from you."

"I don't remember mine," Arianna said.

"You were only an infant." The nun sighed wearily. "She missed you both very much. Every night she cried for her babies."

There was a strained silence as Arianna and Vicki read the birth certificates to find clues to this mystery.

"This doesn't prove much," Vicki insisted. "It simply proves that my father lied about my mother's name."

"You don't believe that," the nun said.

"Where is Francesca?" Arianna asked.

"She's gone." Mother Teresa's voice broke. "And I don't know where."

* * *

The most expensive room at the Orange Motel on Route 82 in New Jersey was furnished with plastic. Only the television set reflected authenticity. It was a Sony nineteen-inch color set, and it was tuned to "All My Children." The scenes shifted rapidly as the room's two occupants spoke.

"I didn't kill Giotti."

Tony's pointed chin thrust forward as he spoke, and his high cheekbones flushed with anger. He stared at Francesca with intensity. She was still very beautiful. Her body was slim, and her green eyes shone with more passion than he remembered.

"God's finally punishing you, Tony," she said calmly.

He coughed and quickly covered his mouth with a beautifully ironed handkerchief, which he discreetly rolled up and placed on the dresser.

"You talk like a religious nut. You've been away from the real world too long. From me too long."

He grasped her small hands in his. They felt like silk though she worked in the convent's gardens. He looked at her face for evidence of the passing years, but there were no lines around her eyes. Time had stood still for Francesca. The only evidence that she was not the same woman he had left at the airport was a new look of strength in her eyes.

He returned to his point. "I won't go to prison for something I haven't done."

"There's a way to avoid trouble," Francesca said.

"What's that? Prayer?"

Abruptly, Tony released her hands and walked to the bar. He poured a shot of scotch, drank it, and coughed.

"You never could drink," she said dryly. "You had none of the bad habits of a mobster. That's why I loved you. Except for your business, you were a decent man."

She took several long breaths.

"All these years it's haunted me that I didn't feel you were capable of doing anything wrong. I'd remind myself of how you used me to manipulate George, how you knew the Don would be murdered at our baby's baptism, how you stole her from me. Finally I realized that you were rotten to the core. I was so stupid not to see that."

Her face was alive with rage. He grabbed her roughly, and her blue silk shirt tore. He kissed her hard. Surprised that her response was cool, he released her as if she had a disease.

"So," he said wearily, "you don't love me any longer."

"I do love you, Tony. But it's not the same."

"What other way is there for a man and woman to love?"

"We can be friends."

"Friends are for drinking and playing golf," he said nastily. He pushed his dyed hair back from his brow.

"You're Arianna's father. I'm here because of her."

"She doesn't need you."

"The media will cause trouble. They'll find out about me, and it will be a great shock for Arianna and Victoria Regina."

"So it's your daughters and not me that you're worried about."

"I care about all of us," she said.

"I don't believe you. You want revenge for my taking Arianna."

"At the beginning I did. But life has punished you enough. I'm here to protect my children. One of them is our daughter. Do you want her to be dragged through slime when she's about to marry the man she loves?"

"Arianna never listens to me," he complained. "She's stubborn, like you."

"Tony, what are you going to do about the Giotti mess?"

"The lawyers will tell me when it's safe to return home."

"There's another way to prove your innocence."

"And that is?"

"We must find the killer. Do you have any ideas?"

He looked thoughtful as he took a toothpick from a box on the table. He put the toothpick between his teeth and ground it to a pulp. When he was finished he put the splinters in an ashtray.

"Someone in the organization hates me," he said.

"Who?"

"The killings have a pattern that doesn't ring true."

"The killings? Are there more than one?"

He nodded. "They're too personal. Like the attack on Arianna."

"Which killings are you talking about?" she asked.

"Maria Cortese."

"But that was long ago."

"It was never solved."

"Who else?"

"Your friend."

Francesca's eyes opened wide. "Jamie?"

"The police think it was a Mafia hit. But I had nothing to do with it."

"Except for George, the victims have been women," she observed.

"Yes, and if Arianna was killed she'd be a third. This is not Mafia business. This is personal. That's why I don't want you to go to the media. Whoever is out there might be looking for you."

"I'm not going to hide any longer. I want to meet my daughters."

"This is not the right time, Francesca," he warned.

"You're wrong, Tony. It is the right time. No one— not you, not this hidden assassin—is going to keep me from Arianna and Victoria Regina."

Chapter 35

As Vicki drove by, Manhattan's Upper West Side was teaming with street hustlers. There were more than two dozen of them strung along upper Broadway, cups out, hard-luck stories ready. Some held cardboard signs, and others relied on their emaciated faces to convey their desperate need for money.

Dismayed, Vicki swung down Sixty-second Street. On one corner three crack dealers were making a sale. Her immediate response was a desire to confront them.

Two policemen walked toward the dealers, yet the dealers didn't register fear; they knew the police had no clout on the streets. When her father was a cop it had been different. Crooks were afraid of cops. Crooks were bad. Cops were good. Right was right and wrong was wrong. Crimes had to be punished.

Arianna was correct. Vicki was not particularly compassionate.

Traffic was heavy on Ninth Avenue. The tunnel area was a hangout for prostitutes, working girls dressed in leather. Working girls who felt nothing for the johns.

She was like them. She paid Paul for sex. When he asked to see her again she refused. Like the working girls, she wanted no emotional strings.

As Vicki turned onto Fourteenth Street she concentrated on Mother Teresa's words. Arianna Tucci was her blood sister—the daughter of the man she hated.

And Francesca Cella was her blood mother.

Impossible!

When she arrived home Vicki phoned two smart and efficient detectives. She made a date for the next morning. Then she took out the card that Arianna had given her. She dialed.

Arianna drove down the West Side Highway without her normal speed because her vision was blurry. When she left the convent Arianna had been trembling with excitement.

What was Francesca like? What could Arianna say to her? What did Francesca look like? Was there a resemblance?

When she reached the Village she parked in front of her town house. Inside, she checked her messages.

Robert hadn't called. After he had announced their marriage the media went haywire. Robert went out of town without telling her. She dialed his office. His secretary said he hadn't returned.

When the phone rang she picked it up and heard Vicki Giotti's voice.

"I've made an appointment at ten A.M. with two detectives. Do you want to be there?" Vicki said brusquely.

"That's pretty early for me to make sense."

There was a silence, but Arianna sensed Vicki's intolerance. Then Vicki said, "Do you or don't you?"

"Tell me where."

She wrote down the information and heard an abrupt click. Arianna shivered. They were less than two years apart, yet Arianna felt that Vicki was from another era.

Vicki was a law-and-order woman. Arianna was a woman who believed in freedom. What could they have in common?

There was someone she must speak to. Arianna changed clothes, then walked two blocks to Nanna's apartment.

Every morning Antoinette brushed her long white hair for half an hour and pinned it up in a chignon. Then she washed her face with icy water. Her complexion was healthy. Though she was in her seventies, her lips still bore a pink glow.

She sat at her window, sipped coffee, and planned her day. She moved slowly, so everything took longer. Yet she insisted on the daily rituals. She shopped for food, spoke to neighbors, visited church, and returned home to cook supper.

She used to attend the church bingo, but everyone made a fuss because she was Tony's mother. She stopped attending because she wanted a quiet, dignified life. Let Tony and Arianna enjoy the glamour.

There was a knock on the door. Antoinette wondered who it was. She looked carefully through the peephole and saw her granddaughter. When she opened the door she noticed that Arianna was dressed in a simple skirt and blouse.

"What's wrong? Are you sick?" Antoinette asked, holding her palm to Arianna's forehead. Arianna felt feverish, and she'd been crying. "Trouble with your boyfriend?"

"That's not why I'm here."

She sounded odd as she walked into the living room and sat on a chair.

"I have to speak to you," Arianna said.

Antoinette sensed this was going to be bad. She had lived through other such moments in her life and recognized the signposts.

"Tell me," she said calmly.

"Nanna, you wouldn't lie to me."

Antoinette shook her head. "What's wrong?"

"Is my mother alive?"

Antoinette heard a strange ringing as her head pounded and her heartbeat quickened. This was the question she had prayed Arianna would never ask. If she answered truthfully, her son would never forgive her. But she couldn't lie to her granddaughter.

"Who told you?"

"Mother Teresa, at the Convent of the Sacred Heart in Peekskill. I went there this morning."

"How did you know about the convent?"

"Mother Teresa sent for me. She told me that my mother is alive. She's lived all these years at the convent, working in the gardens." Arianna began crying again. "How could my father do this to me?"

"Arianna, darling," Antoinette said slowly, "your

father was afraid for your safety. Things happened between him and your mother. I don't know what they were. But he was afraid that she would take you away."

"So he tells me she's dead?"

"I told him it was the wrong thing to do, but he wouldn't listen to me. You know how he is. He thinks he's the only one who knows what's right. He loves you so. He only did it for you."

"He let me grow up alone, all those years, when I had a mother. I can't believe it."

"Francesca always loved you, Arianna. She wrote to me all these years."

Arianna's eyes grew round with disbelief.

"You were in contact with her? How could you keep this from me?"

"I had to, for Tony's sake. I'm his mother."

"I'm his daughter, but I hate him."

"Don't insult your father. He has his reasons."

But Arianna was shouting. "His reasons! He kept my mother from me. He made me think I was responsible because she died when I was born. How do you think I felt about that?" She paused, breathing hard. "What about Vicki Giotti? Mother Teresa said that we are sisters. Is that true?"

Antoinette bowed her head with grief.

"Does everyone know?" Arianna demanded.

"A few people know."

"My aunts and uncles? My cousins? Is that why my father never wanted me to be friendly with them?"

"He was protecting you," Antoinette insisted.

"He's always protecting me. Well, he'll pay for that."

"Your father is in trouble. You must stand by him."

"He wants the life of a mobster, so let him stew," Arianna shouted.

"Then you met your mother?" Antoinette asked.

"No."

"I thought you went to the convent."

"Yes, I did. So did Vicki Giotti."

"Then?"

"Francesca wasn't there. She's disappeared."

❧ *Chapter 36* ❧

*I*t began like many affairs, on a lush silk sofa in a private Waldorf Astoria suite where two pleated lampshades colored the room with a soft lavender hue. He drank scotch before dinner, and she ordered champagne. They dined on terrine of warm foie gras in a truffle sauce, potato puree with chopped chives, tortelloni in crust with dried mushrooms, grilled duck with curried orange mayonnaise, and grape sorbet.

The dessert cart was rolled in and elegant pastries and espresso served. He ordered more scotch, and she ordered a liquor from Tuscany.

The waiter lowered his eyes, removed the portable dining table, and left the dessert, coffee, and drinks on the marble coffee table.

They sat in silence. She was a glamorous woman who had educated herself. Her jewels were breathtaking. Around her neck she wore a gold and mother-of-pearl collar with black onyx, pavé diamonds, and blue and pink tourmalines. On her earlobes were matching diamond earrings. Her ring was a blue diamond with two trilliants, designed by Harry Winston.

Like her jewels, her life-style was a magnificent creation. She had completely transformed herself and traveled in European circles, hungry for the education that a wealthy but socially outcast childhood lacked. Now she exuded charm, elegant bearing, and the symbols of wealth.

But the one thing she craved still eluded her. Power.

She was born to a powerful man and had married a powerful man, and if she were male she would inherit the mantle of power. She had all the other necessary traits. She was smart, cruel, and a killer.

Only she was a woman.

Growing up, she hated this one undeniable fact that eliminated her from royal succession. When her father was assassinated she planned for the time when she could take over his power base.

It took years of patience and planning, which she spent changing her image. She steeped herself in elegant fashions from Milan. Simple tailored outfits for daytime. Eccentric color combinations at night. Tonight she wore one of those creations, a strapless chiffon that hugged her svelte figure and complemented her fabulous jewelry.

She looked like a contessa. She had royal wealth and beauty. She wanted more.

The slim man with graying sideburns was attentive. His sharp eyes darted about the room during the private dinner, wondering why he was there. Finally, during the main course, he realized what she was orchestrating and what his reward might be. Still, he was startled when she made her bold move.

"I need a second in command. The man I choose will have unequaled authority. Only I will be above him," she explained in a purring voice.

"Why me?" he asked bluntly. Slowly he sipped scotch as he watched her twirl the whipped cream from a peach tart with her tongue, sending a message of lust.

"I like you."

"The truth, please."

She sipped espresso. Then she put the cup down deliberately.

He found his senses sharpen in his admiration for her.

"You are close to Tony. You know his secrets."

"His secrets are known to several men," he answered carefully.

"Some aren't. I have to be sure of those before I move on him."

"But you have moved on him already, haven't you, Signora?"

She smiled. He was sending the compliment that he had already identified her diabolical scheme.

"There is much more to be done."

Indulgently, she watched him, noticing the shape of his head as he turned away and the tormented smile on his face when Tony's name was mentioned. Divided loyalties, she thought.

"You've known Tony for a very long time."

"I was a street kid, and now I'm a gentleman. Everything I know and am, Tony taught me. He in-

sisted that I change. That's how he is. When he wants
something, he makes it happen.''

"I know. My father was one of his victims."

"You think Tony engineered his murder?"

"Now who's being dishonest?" She patted the
space on the couch next to her. "Come here," she
said.

"Signora, this is business."

"Of course," she agreed. "But business is a terribly
intimate thing. Isn't it?"

"I don't think so."

Her eyebrows rose at his denial of her invitation.
She pulled off her exquisite collar and placed it on the
table. Provocatively, she removed one earring, then
the other. Her green eyeshadow seemed to darken to
match her mood.

"Come here," she commanded.

He shrugged his shoulders, put down the scotch,
and walked slowly to the couch. He stood before her,
waiting. She reached up and slapped him hard on the
face.

"If you're going to be my second in command, you
must learn to follow orders."

He stood his ground.

"I'm not a whore," he said.

"You're bought and paid for," she scoffed.

She pulled him toward her. When he was beside her
she kissed him, her lips parting his, her tongue exploring his mouth. Her hands reached inside his silk shirt
and fondled his nipples. She tossed aside the gold
chains on his chest. Then she placed her lips upon his
nipples and sucked them until he moaned. Without
ceremony she took his hands and placed them under

her beautiful formal gown. He groaned, feeling her bare body beneath the silk.

"So?" She took her lips from his body. "You seem to like what you've found."

Her vagina was moist and hot as his fingers explored her industriously. His other hand disrobed her. A touch at the zipper and the gown fell, revealing her beautiful body. Her soft skin was flecked with gold sequin pasties. On her nipples they formed a provocative design.

"Madonna," he swore as he kissed the jeweled nipples.

She groped at his trousers and felt his hardness. Quickly, she unzipped his fly and took out his throbbing organ. She put her mouth on it and sucked him thirstily. His hands held her breasts. Then he put his lips on them. Trembling, he turned her around and placed her flat on the sofa.

"I want you this way," he said.

He inserted his penis from behind, slipping quickly into her wetness. Her vagina felt supple as he pushed into her. His penis was hard and grew harder still. The provocative motions stimulated him. He opened his mouth in agony as she pushed her buttocks toward him, granting him further entrance into her body.

"Give it to me hard," she whispered.

"But—"

"Like a *putana*," she ordered.

Granted permission, he entered her roughly, the motion tearing at her genital area. But she did not ask him to stop. Instead she pushed herself toward him, craving stimulation. She cried out. He stopped, but she pushed against him again. She began a series of screams like an animal in pain. He kept pumping her as if she were a woman of the streets. Her screams became more guttural as she cursed God.

He waited. When she stopped screaming he came all over her, and his semen emptied on the expensive couch.

Shivering, she moved away, but he pulled her back. He put her hands on his limp penis and commanded her to manipulate him. She worked him hard until his organ was hot again. Sweat pouring from his brow, he climaxed, calling her a whore and a bitch. She came again and again, his manipulation exciting her as well.

Finally, their bodies exhausted, there was a silence as they resumed normal breathing. She moved away from him quickly. With a silk handkerchief she wiped her face, her breasts, and her vagina.

She opened her purse, took out a miniature mirror, and tucked back the wisps of glorious, honey-colored hair that had fallen free from the jeweled combs.

She looked at him. His eyes were slanted and conveyed darkness.

"Have I passed your test?" he asked angrily.

Her eyes grew flirtatious as she laughed. She grabbed his organ and squeezed it until she caused him pain, but he didn't react.

"You will do," she said. "But remember always, I am *la prima mafiosa*."

Chapter 37

*T*he lunch crowd at Mezzogiorno spoke softly, influenced by the elegant Florentine interiors that were a marked contrast to the area. The daytime atmosphere at Mezzogiorno ignored the commercial modern city. Replicas of medieval prints hung on its walls. A sculpture of a sun god was placed prominently in the foyer. It was a symbol of midday, Mezzogiorno's meaning in the Italian language.

On the ceiling were large printed letters from an archaic form of Italian. Similar words were reproduced on the menu.

Vito Marchese smiled as he tried to translate the words. "This is difficult," he groaned. "We didn't study this version at Brooklyn College."

"You have to be a scholar specializing in antiquity to decipher it," Vicki said.

"A scholar I'm not."

His brown eyes gazed at her earnestly. Vicki knew that Vito suffered from low self-esteem, as she did.

"Stop berating yourself. Aren't you the star of the district attorney's office?"

He grasped her hand. "Only since you've been on leave. When are you coming back to work? I miss you."

"I need more time. My father's murder really blew me away."

"That's a tough one, but you've always been so driven. How can you stay at home and do nothing?"

"What's new?" Vicki asked, changing the subject.

"We don't think that Tucci had anything to do with your father's murder."

"You mean he didn't pull the trigger."

Vito shook his head. "No. The murder was ordered by another family member. There are lots of rumblings in the Tucci family. Tony always controlled his soldiers with an iron fist, but there's talk that his street power is eroding. Because he's preoccupied with Atlantic City and Las Vegas, he hasn't given much attention to Lower Manhattan. And the people there resent it."

"I thought his buddy Joey Morro covered that territory for him."

"Funny thing about Joey. He's quite the gentleman now. The wiseguys aren't comfortable shooting the breeze with someone wearing Giorgio Armani suits."

"I thought they liked glamour."

"Only the conservative kind. They're living in the past, when a dark British serge was the epitome of wealth and class. Tony wears those kinds of clothes. But Joey's unisex look is interpreted by the street hoods as queer. They're calling him a pansy."

"What does this mean to the Tucci family?"

"Something's going down. Tucci is hiding out for more than one reason. He's furious at the attack on his daughter. Mike the Crab and Benny the Pill follow her around nowadays."

"Who's guarding Tony?"

"He isn't telling anyone where he is. But Tony can take care of himself. He's a good shot."

"Does anyone know where he is?"

A sudden flicker in his eyes told Vicki that he knew something he couldn't divulge. Before she could pursue it a young waiter interrupted their conversation.

"Would you like to order?"

"Vicki?"

"Crabmeat salad."

"I'll have the carpaccio," Vito said.

The waiter bowed.

"On a diet?" Vito asked.

"I'm watching my weight."

"Why? You're very slim."

Before she could answer his eyes grew troubled. He grasped her hands in his. "Vicki, you're very important to me."

She looked into his dark eyes and trembled.

"Don't," she whispered.

But he continued. "I know you've been working with the Abused Children's Project, so your father must have been difficult. I know something about that. I didn't have to hassle with that problem. I went to college and law school. My sister wants to attend college, and my father is against it. He gives her a hard time. So I pay her tuition. But I'm scared to death that she's going to end up on drugs or something worse."

He swallowed hard. This was a mouthful for Vito. Outside of the courtroom he was usually quiet.

"So Vicki, I know things can be hard. But life can improve with the right guy."

She was touched by his announcement of caring and felt soft and loving. Defensively, she searched for the tough part of herself, the part that she counted on to pull her through anything, the part that needed no one. But she couldn't grasp it.

She felt shaky as warmth filled her body with enormous vitality. Suddenly she realized that she cared more for Vito than she had suspected.

"You do care. I can see it in your eyes," he said happily.

"You've always been good to me."

"I could be better," he said flirtatiously.

"There are things you don't know."

"Must I know them?"

"Some."

"Tell me what you have to, Vicki. But what you want to keep to yourself is fine. I trust you."

She waited. Then she signaled the waiter and ordered wine. Silence reigned as Vito stared deeply into her eyes. When the wine arrived she held up her glass.

"To you, Vito. You've melted down the cold bitch of Jane Street," she said bitterly.

He grabbed her free hand as he raised his glass.

"Not a cold bitch. Never a cold bitch. Just someone who's been hurt."

Feelings of caring and trust flooded Vicki. She wanted Vito to know everything.

"I have to tell you—"

"Don't talk now," he whispered.

"No," she protested.

"Okay. What?"

"I'm pregnant."

He was caught by surprise. He expected information from her past, statements about her sadness, even perhaps about abuse, but never this. His eyes reflected immediate pain. He put down the glass, gingerly picked up his fork and stared at his salad as if it were loaded with arsenic. His complexion turned white, and his eyes lost their intensity.

"I didn't know you have someone," he finally said.

"I don't."

He looked up, puzzled. "Then—"

"I hired a surrogate."

He dropped his fork. *"What?"*

"I paid a man to impregnate me because I want a baby. I didn't want a man, so it seemed a sensible method."

"You mean you didn't care for him at all?"

"No."

He fidgeted. He had no preparation for this type of information, and it hit him hard. He was furious at her.

"How could you?"

"Why are you taking this as a personal insult?" she asked.

"Because it is," he stormed. "You let a stranger make love to you . . . someone you have no feelings for. It's not right."

"It's my right. And I'm carrying my baby because of it."

His face contorted. There was a wildness there that she'd seen in court when he lost a major case and his cool demeanor changed to primitive fury.

He wanted to slap her. She'd spoiled all his dreams for the future.

"Vicki, how could you?" he accused her again.

In silence they stared at each other. Vicki waited, telling herself that this man with hate written on his face was not Vito.

Angrily, he reached into his pocket. He threw bills at the center of the table. Then he stormed out of the calm, beautiful interior into the most complicated city in the world.

Arianna waited impatiently for Vicki. Vicki had changed the appointment with the detectives to three P.M. Arianna arrived promptly to discover Vicki was not there.

The receptionist at Mulright and Caller was young. She wore a pink dress, pink shoes, and a pink carnation in her hair. Arianna thought she looked like Billie Holliday.

"Ms. Giotti is usually punctual," the young woman said.

When Vicki finally arrived her hair was windblown and her green outfit was short, sassy, and smart.

Arianna whistled. "A date with a man?"

"So?" Vicki retorted.

"Vicki, let's talk. We don't need this meeting."

Ignoring her, Vicki turned to the receptionist. "Where are they?"

"They're in court. You know how that is."

Vicki looked annoyed.

"Why don't we have coffee?" Arianna suggested.

"I've had coffee."

Arianna felt her temper rise as she walked over to her sister. "I have to talk to you," she said bluntly.

"Okay." Vicki turned to the receptionist. "When the crew comes in, tell them we'll be right back. Lead on," she said to Arianna.

They waited for the elevator in silence. In the elevator Vicki looked stressed.

"Can't you relax?" Arianna said.

Vicki shot her a hateful look. She was always angry at Arianna. What had Arianna done? Nothing. Except be the daughter of Tony Tucci.

In the lobby Vicki pointed to a coffee shop. It was past lunch hour, so the place was empty. They sat in a booth and ordered coffee.

"I have news," Arianna began.

Vicki put three sugars in her coffee. "I like sugar," she said defensively.

"We are sisters," Arianna announced excitedly. "My grandmother confirmed it all. My mother—I mean *our* mother—was married to your father. She left him for my father."

"Oh, I see. She left a cop for a mobster. Great lady."

"I don't know exactly what happened. Your father wouldn't let Francesca keep you. She tried."

"She didn't try very hard. She didn't go to court."

"Nanna says because she married my father, court wasn't a good idea." Arianna waited, then added, "I guess we are sisters."

Her colorful fingernails tapped a rhythm on the table. One nail sported a red heart. Another, a gold star. Vicki looked at Arianna's fingernails with distaste. She compared them with her short, clean, and unpolished nails.

"I still want the detectives to investigate," Vicki insisted.

"Okay. I'll go along with that."

"This Francesca person left my father and me because she fell in love with your father. Is that the story?"

"Guess so."

Vicki felt an anger that was deep and scary. She had always hated Tony Tucci because he was Mafia. Her feelings toward him toughened after her father's murder. Now she had more reason to despise him, if he had taken her beautiful mother away from her.

"We have to talk about our mother," Arianna said passionately. "She's had a rough time. When we find her we must make things easier for her. Don't you agree?"

"This is pretty new to me. I can't turn myself on and off. It's going to take a while to think about this." Vicki paused, then asked, "How do you feel about her?"

"I'm dying to meet her. Aren't you?"

"I don't know—"

"Vicki, can we make a pact?" Arianna interrupted.

"What kind of pact?"

"Can we be friends?"

"I'm going to put your father in jail. How can we be friends?"

"But he's not guilty."

"Maybe he didn't do this particular killing, but he's been responsible for many others." Vicki paused thoughtfully. "My life is about law and order. I grew up that way. My father was a cop. How can you expect us to be friends when I'm trying to put your father away for murder?"

Then, with a quick flourish, she picked up the check. She paid for the coffee and disappeared, leaving Arianna to dwell sadly on what had been said.

❧ *Chapter 38* ❧

*D*arling, I've missed you," Arianna whispered as Robert drew her close.

"Sorry, sweetheart. I had to retreat. Went back to the Maine homestead. Walked by the lake. Played tennis at the club. Needed to get back to my roots. One morning I woke up remembering how lovely you are. I caught the next plane back."

He wound his arms around her and kissed her passionately. "Sorry I didn't call, but I had to sort out my priorities."

"What kind of priorities?" she asked.

"Can I handle the notoriety of being married to a famous rock star? It's one thing to work for abused children—even my friends at the Yale Club say one or two good words about that. But being followed around by reporters who ask personal questions is really difficult."

"Maybe we shouldn't marry."

Slowly, Arianna walked to the other side of the study. The room was cluttered but she knew where everything was. She picked up a pillow, propped it against the plush couch, and sat.

Arianna wore a short dress of nude silk jersey that hugged her body. Her lovely legs were crossed, and she wore a gold snake bracelet around one ankle. A matching necklace lay at her throat with the snake pointed to the cleavage of her magnificent breasts. Her beautiful blue eyes were highlighted by intense gold eyeshadow.

Robert walked to the couch, aching to love her. But she resisted.

"Don't. Lots has happened in a few days. My life's been completely turned around."

"Nothing's happened to us?"

"I'm not certain about us. I have loyalties—to my father, my family. You're not going to be able to hide your head in the sand if you marry me. You've led a protected life—your background, the sailboats, the clubs. Can you handle this kind of life?"

"Our life doesn't always have to be public."

She shook her head angrily. "Not in theory. But it's like living in the center of a hurricane. I've lived with notoriety all my life, and it's hard to avoid. When I was baptized, Don Allegro was shot. I was an infant and witnessed one of the most violent crimes ever committed in this city. Being my father's daughter has robbed me of any privacy."

Her porcelain face registered outrage at the way fate demanded that she must live. An unseen danger always lurked in the background. Her shadows, her father's men, were guardian angels or devils, depending on her mood.

She tore a pasted gold heart from her cheek, looking at it as if she didn't know what it was. Her skin's golden sheen conveyed abundant energy. She glowed with life. But she wore an expression he couldn't decipher. To add to the mystery, she swirled her lion's mane so that her hair covered half her face. Then her lips set into a Mona Lisa smile.

He sensed he must save their love now or it would be gone. He sat beside her, careful not to touch her.

"I agree. You're the center of controversy. The media documents your every move, along with your father's career. But you're wrong to think you don't love him. You love him very much. I can see that in your expression whenever his name is mentioned."

"I may love him, but I don't approve of him," she insisted.

"We can't always approve of the people we love." He took her hand gently, kissed it, and placed it next to his heart. "Love ruins our peace and quiet. It breaks up our pretty plans. But we're not born to be perfect. We're born to love each other and to shoot for the moon. You're my moon, Arianna, and I don't want to lose you."

She crumbled under his passionate declaration. He swept her into his arms. They lay on the soft couch and gazed into each other's eyes. He kissed her lips, moved down to her neck, her breasts, her body. Then he retraced his route, ending at her soft, lovely lips again.

He removed her clothes, then his own. Quickly, he began a sweeping motion that sent waves of love to her. She held him tightly as he moved into her again and again until exquisite pleasure was triggered.

"Oh, my darling," she moaned.

He kissed her deeply and again guided himself into her. He slid in easily and began a soft motion, afraid that she might be tender. Firmly inside, he thrust again and again until the moment of his ecstasy, when he whispered that he loved her.

Afterward Arianna told Robert her news.

"Your mother alive? Vicki your sister? I can't believe it," Robert exclaimed.

"I haven't met Francesca yet. And Vicki isn't very friendly."

"She's hesitant to open up because of her childhood. Has she told you—"

He stopped in midsentence, remembering that Vicki's pregnancy was a secret.

Arianna didn't notice. "She's hiring detectives even though Nanna told me it's true. Vicki wants proof."

"Vicki believes in facts," Robert agreed.

Arianna's visit to the Convent of the Sacred Heart was reported to Joey Morro by her bodyguards. Joey withheld the information from Tony, analyzing whether it was important. Deciding that it was simply one of Arianna's whims, he finally passed it on to Tony. When he did, a look of shock replaced Tony's calm demeanor. His eyes grew very dark. Joey knew something important had happened.

"When did she visit?" Tony asked Joey.

"Last week."

"What day?"

"Wednesday, I think."

Tony grabbed the lapels of Joey's chic suit.

"You think? Don't you know?"

"It was Wednesday. What's this about?"

"It's personal," Tony said, his hands trembling. "Anything else?"

Joey conveyed news of business dealings but realized that Tony was preoccupied.

After the meeting Tony said, "I'm moving from this spot. I'll let you know where I am."

"But you're safe here."

"Remember, when you hide out you must move around."

"Tony, you need bodyguards."

"Look, when I was a kid on the streets I didn't need anyone. I'm still that tough guy," he said, taking a gun from his pocket.

"You shouldn't carry that," Joey cautioned.

"I'm ready for any son of a bitch who wants to try to take me. Let them come. I'll blow their heads off. Now go. I'll call you."

After Joey left, Tony collapsed. Francesca was right. He must give himself up. He must explain things to Arianna. She must know about her mother. Why else would she visit the convent?

As night fell Tony's spirits sank. In the last few years his relationship with Arianna had soured. If she discovered he had lied to her about her mother's death, it might be impossible to reach her.

Tony's head bowed as an enormous sadness exhausted him. He had banished the only woman he'd ever loved for Arianna's safety. Now he might lose his beloved daughter's love forever.

He looked into the barrel of his gun and wondered why he should go on living.

Chapter 39

Arianna awoke with a contented heart. Alongside her, in his sleep, Robert murmured, "Arianna." Watching him, Arianna felt lucky. Tears sprang to her eyes. Robert was everything to her. His love for her was startling. Hers for him was miraculous. Fate had decided to be generous at last.

She ached to see her mother and remembered moments when she was very young. There was a touch, a sense, a smell, a love she had thought was gone forever.

That's why her songs were about lost love. Now Robert's love had changed her. She felt generous about love. She hoped her audience would love her new songs as much as they loved her songs of loss.

The phone rang. She picked it up quickly, not wanting to disturb Robert.

"Arianna."

Her father's voice sounded strange.

"What's wrong, Papa?" she asked.

"Can you ever forgive me?"

"I don't know," she said honestly.

"I don't blame you, Arianna."

"Papa, are you all right?"

"Goodbye, my lovely," Tony Tucci said.

Trembling, Arianna walked into the motel room. At her side Robert fended off reporters. Behind her large sunglasses Arianna's eyes were puffy. She had cried for hours, blaming herself.

After her father's call she'd phoned Joey and begged him to take her to her father. Angrily, he replied that her phone was tapped and hung up. Again she tried to reach her father's people but was not successful. A few hours later the police called.

"Your father is dead," said a man who identified himself as Detective James L. Murphy. Then he told her where Tony's body had been found.

"Who killed him?"

"We suspect suicide," the detective said somberly.

Arianna fell apart after that. During the long ride to the motel Robert tried to comfort her.

"He always handled the police. I don't believe he'd commit suicide," Arianna insisted.

"He may have felt terrible because you discovered the truth about your mother."

"I tried to tell him—no, I didn't tell him. I should have told him—I forgive him. He might be alive if I had said that."

"Arianna, you mustn't blame yourself."

When she walked into the motel room everything

was neatly organized. Her father had died the way he lived.

His body was lying in the center of a large double bed, dressed in a blue silk robe and slippers. Alongside his dead body the sheets were stained with blood. Drops of blood were on the carpet also.

The room was crowded with detectives documenting Tony Tucci's death.

In a corner of the room a petite woman waited quietly. Her beautiful face was drawn, and her lovely green eyes were filled with tears. Next to her a detective was asking questions.

Curiously, Arianna looked at the woman.

Suddenly she knew. Trembling, she walked toward her.

The woman's face lit up as she opened her arms.

"My beautiful Arianna," Francesca said. "My baby."

"*Mother?*"

"Yes, Arianna. Your mother is here. I will *never* leave you again."

❧ *Chapter 40* ❧

*T*ony's death had a disastrous effect on the East Coast Mafia families. Divisions were widespread, and wholesale assassinations occurred. When things quieted down Sally Allegro Solari assumed control of the Tucci family with Joey Morro at her side.

Her plan had taken more than thirty years to succeed. It had begun when Tony resisted Sally's charms. Insulted, she formulated a plan her father, Don Allegro, would be proud of.

First, to kill Tony's mistress.

Second, to kill Tony's wife; but since Francesca disappeared before Sally accomplished this, she killed her friend, Jamie, as a warning.

Third, to kill George Giotti. Luckily for Sally, George had taken Tony's gun, stolen years earlier, to the scene of the crime.

Fourth, to kill Arianna.

And last, to kill Tony.

She had accomplished three out of five.

But now that Tony was dead, Arianna and Francesca didn't matter anymore.

For she was the unchallenged queen. Ironically, the machismo of the Mafia wouldn't let her go public. Secretly, she was *la prima mafiosa*. To consolidate her power, she announced that she was marrying Joey Morro.

Vito Marchese's informants whispered about Sally's audacious actions. He conveyed this information to the local police. But Tony's suicide was executed faultlessly, so the police wouldn't consider that it was an assassination.

When Vito phoned Vicki about his suspicions she sounded defeated, which surprised him.

"Vicki, when you return to the office we can goad the boss to pursue this. I'm sure that Sally killed your dad."

"It's not important," Vicki said.

"I thought you wanted to find your father's murderer."

"My father's photo is plastered all over the media along with Tucci's. The damned TV stations cover it every night as if it were international news. When are they going to drop it?"

"The Mafia is popular. Isn't that the reason we pursued this case? Mafia makes careers."

"Let it make yours, Vito."

"What's wrong with you? You were always the most driven of us all."

"I'm going to be a mother. That's the most important thing in my life."

"But your career—your work! That's important,
too."

"After the baby is born I have to rethink my goals.
I don't want to be away from home when my baby
needs me. I want to be there while my child is growing
up."

"Vicki, you won't be happy just being a mother,"
he said sharply.

"I think being a mother is the most wonderful thing
in the world."

Vito felt as if he were speaking to someone he'd
never met. He felt guilty that his feelings for Vicki had
switched violently after learning that she was pregnant
by a stranger.

"Good luck," Vito said.

"Goodbye, Vito."

At the weekly conference Vito told his boss that he
definitely wanted to continue the Tucci investigation.

Vicki broke off her conversation with Vito. Law and
order didn't interest her. Her baby was the most
important thing in the world, and she decided she must
change her life.

Several times Arianna phoned to ask if Vicki would
meet Francesca. Vicki refused. Then Robert dropped
by.

"Vicki, you're blaming your mother, and that's not
fair to Francesca. Your father was a tormented man.
He hurt your mother badly. She was taken to the
hospital. When she wanted to return for you, he
threatened her."

"That's not the way I see it. My mother had the hots for a mafioso and left me. I can't forgive her," Vicki said stormily.

Robert cautioned her. "Abused children have a hard time because they expect people to be perfect. They've been hurt by their parents when they were too small to cope. When they grow up they search for people who won't hurt them. But nobody's perfect. I'm not. Neither is Arianna. She's afraid of being hurt, like you are. But we can't live our lives waiting for perfect people. There are none."

He kissed her affectionately. "Vicki, don't you want your baby to enter this life surrounded by people who love her?" Vicki nodded. "Then forgive your mother. She loves you. And Arianna wants to be a real sister to you. It's important to her. It's important to me."

"Robert, you've always been wonderful to me, but I can't seem to change . . . though I often want to. I tried with Vito."

"What happened?"

"He wanted to marry me. When I told him how I became pregnant he walked out," she said sadly.

"Don't let the fact that Vito has limitations stop you from opening yourself to life. Search your heart, Vicki, and you'll find a deep love for your mother."

"Thanks for coming over, Robert."

After he left she thought about what he'd said. It was true. She had a strong memory of the woman who had sung to her when she was a baby. She remembered her fragrance . . . her softness . . . her love.

Then it was gone. The only thing remaining was the harshness of her father's love.

"Mother?" Vicki cried out in her sleep. She was in

Francesca's arms, and her mother told her all was safe. When she woke up she was drenched in perspiration.

Time passed quickly. A fall mist covered Manhattan and rain covered the streets daily. Vicki would walk the streets and watch the homeless people wrapped in rags. Often she felt like them, though she lived in a luxury apartment house.

One day the news she had feared broke. On the five o'clock news Mary Adams revealed the astonishing fact that Mrs. Tony Tucci had once been Mrs. George Giotti. She added that Arianna Tucci, the rock star, and Vicki Giotti, the assistant district attorney, were half sisters and that George Giotti's murder was probably motivated by personal reasons, although the authorities denied this.

Vicki packed two bags and fled Manhattan before the media could get to her.

✤ *Chapter 41* ✤

*T*he Convent of the Sacred Heart was a wonderful retreat for Vicki. Because she had to justify Vicki's presence, Mother Teresa gave Vicki a job in the office. Though she was not religious, when Vicki heard the sisters sing hymns as she walked in the gardens she felt at peace.

Mother Teresa promised that her presence would be kept secret, so Arianna's visit came as a surprise.

"We've been frantic about you," Arianna said.

Her wild mane was sculpted simply about her porcelain face. Though she wore no makeup, Arianna looked gorgeous.

"How did you know I was here?" Vicki asked.

"I guessed. Are you okay?"

"I'm not your responsibility."

Arianna looked at her older sister. Her sharp nose conveyed a preference for discipline, as did her tone of voice. Her hazel eyes were clear but expressionless. Her flaming red hair was pulled back severely into a tight bun. Her narrow lips and small chin conflicted with her soft body and lovely legs, which were displayed by a short black dress and sandals.

"Vicki, why are you so angry? Mother and I simply want you to be part of our family."

"I don't have a family," Vicki said.

"I'm getting married, Vicki. I'd like you to be there."

"No, I don't think so."

"Don't you ever say anything but no?" Arianna said angrily. "Are you one of those people who are always negative because life isn't going exactly the way you wish? Why must you turn your back on the people who care about you? Here's your chance to begin a new life, Vicki. Mother wants you in her life, and so do I."

"No, thanks."

Arianna stood with her hands on her hips, shaking her head.

"I'm getting married in a couple of months. I'll send you an invitation. I hope you'll come. If not for my sake, then for Robert's."

"Don't expect me."

The months flew by quickly. From Arianna, Mother Teresa learned about Vicki's refusal to attend Arianna's wedding. One morning she asked Vicki to join her for breakfast.

"Vicki, Francesca suffered a great deal because of the men in her life. Must you continue her suffering? Can't you forgive her?"

"I'm sorry, Mother," Vicki said. "I can't seem to change. I want to. But it's impossible."

"Look, my dear, change isn't easy. It doesn't happen by itself. We must force ourselves when we have the chance. This convent is not an escape from life. It's a place for healing wounds. Francesca stayed here until she was strong enough to return to her life. Now you have a wonderful opportunity to do the same thing. Attend your sister's wedding."

Mother Teresa's voice grew increasingly sad. "I've received a letter from Francesca. Every day she relives the trauma of losing you. Can't you see that she loves you?"

"Does she?"

"Vicki, for the sake of your baby you must try to change," the nun said, "and give your child a family."

"You know about the baby?" Vicki said, startled.

"It's obvious that you're pregnant. I assume that you're not marrying the father?" Vicki shook her head negatively. "Please go to Francesca. She's the one person in the world who will understand. She can help you now."

The day was perfect. The sun shone brightly, and the sky was as blue as the bride's eyes. Arianna's dress was of white silk shantung with a ribbon lace bodice. The skirt was long and full, and on her head she wore a pearl tiara. Swirling from the crown, a French lace veil covered her beautiful face. Around her neck was a collar of gold and diamonds that held a ruby-and-sapphire bird of paradise. Francesca had lent Arianna the necklace. It was the only piece of jewelry she'd kept.

Francesca looked stunning in a gown of light green chiffon decorated with darker green sequins.

"Oh, my darling," Francesca said, "you're going to be very happy."

"Hurry, the limo is here," the housekeeper called.

They rushed into the white car. It drove slowly around the corner to St. Anthony's Church. Inside the church a crowd waited to see Tough Tony's daughter marry. Though they protested, the media was kept outside the church, where they waited impatiently to film the rock star.

Vicki had entered the church earlier via the rectory, explaining to the priest that she wanted to avoid the media. She sat in a pew at the rear of the church.

The traditional wedding march filled the church as Arianna entered, fleeing the cameras outside. Because of her father's recent death she chose not to be escorted.

Slowly Arianna walked down the aisle. Because she was a performer, she was at ease. The altar was decorated with her favorite white lilies. Arianna looked around the church to smile at friends and spotted Vicki.

Suddenly she retraced her steps to the rear of the church while puzzled onlookers watched. When she reached Vicki's pew she held out her hand. Slowly Vicki rose. Then, with a wide smile, she took Arianna's hand.

Together they walked to the rear of the church. Nervously Vicki walked down the aisle with her sister. As she reached the first pew her trembling increased when she saw the woman standing there.

Francesca was smiling, and her green eyes shone like two emeralds.

At the foot of the altar Vicki waited as Arianna climbed the steps to stand alongside Robert. The ceremony was very brief. Afterward the bride and groom kissed. Arianna embraced Vicki. Then she escorted her sister to the first pew.

With tears in her eyes Francesca held out her arms.

"Victoria Regina," she whispered.

"You've come back," Vicki said softly.

❧ *Chapter 42* ❧

*T*he months passed swiftly. Arianna insisted that Vicki live at the town house so that she and Francesca could look after her. Francesca was glowing because she and her daughters were together at last. Sometimes it was painful. When Arianna and Vicki talked about their childhood loneliness Francesca spent hours pacing in her bedroom.

The media kept covering the investigation of Tony's suicide. Finally the police announced that Tony had been murdered. A snitch named Frankie Carlo told the authorities that the assassination of Tony Tucci had been planned at the top. When questioned, Joey Morro and his wife, Sally, had an alibi.

"My son could never commit suicide," Antoinette said to Francesca. "It's a sin."

Though her mother-in-law was making an assumption about Tony, Francesca knew she was probably right. Tony could perform brutally in business, but his conscience wouldn't allow him to take his own life.

Francesca told her daughters that they must forget and forgive the past.

"Now we're a family," Francesca said. "Let the media crank out their stories. We'll simply ignore them."

Francesca supported Vicki's decision to be a single mother, though Antoinette made the Sign Of The Cross every time it was mentioned.

"This is not right," she whispered to Francesca. "Your daughter should marry. Every child needs a father."

Francesca steadfastly refused to interfere.

"Whatever Vicki wants is okay with me," she said.

When she conferred with Robert and Arianna, Robert said it was amazing that Vicki could contemplate having a baby.

"I see it as healthy, Francesca," Robert said. "I encouraged her. I thought maybe—well, Vito Marchese seemed to care for her. . . ."

"Until she told him the truth," Arianna said.

Francesca agreed. "There are men like you, Robert, who accept the woman they love as she is. But most men want a woman to be a fantasy. George and Tony didn't love me. They loved a fantasy wife they created. Unfortunately, Vito sounds like that kind of man."

"Vicki doesn't seem to be upset about him," Arianna observed.

Robert said, "Vicki is sure her dreams won't come true."

"I'm going to do everything I can for Vicki," Arianna vowcd.

Arianna furnished the town house study as a temporary nursery. She shopped at F.A.O. Schwarz and bought loads of toys and stuffed animals. Vicki protested, but Arianna couldn't help herself from wanting to spoil the baby.

Francesca concentrated on the linen, the crib, the diapers, and other necessities. Vicki felt pampered for the first time in her life. When her time came it was five A.M. Arianna and Francesca escorted Vicki to St. Vincent's Hospital while Robert picked up Antoinette. For two hours the family paced in the waiting room. Finally the doctor appeared.

"Your daughter has given birth to a girl," he said to Francesca.

Francesca and Arianna kissed each other, giddy with happiness.

"May I see her?" Francesca asked.

"You may go in," the doctor said.

"And the baby?"

"She's in the nursery. Ask the nurse to show her to you," he said.

The family walked down the hospital corridor and stopped at the nursery. When the nurse held out a tiny bundle, Antoinette began crying.

"She looks like Vicki," Francesca said.

"No, she looks like you," Arianna said.

"She looks like both of you," Robert added.

They giggled. When they went into Vicki's room she looked tired but happy.

"Darling, she's beautiful," Francesca said. "You and Arianna were beautiful babies, too."

"To our family," Arianna whispered, kissing her sister's cheek.

Judith Michael

America's New Sensational Novelist

Judith Michael knows what you want to read. She burst on to the scene with her bestselling novel DECEPTIONS, bringing us every woman's ultimate fantasy...to live another woman's life for just a little while. She swept us away with POSSESSIONS, a sophisticated, poignant novel of love and illusion, loyalty and betrayal, society and family. And now Judith Michael brings us into the seductive, secretive world of PRIVATE AFFAIRS.